Evil Brew

Evil Brew

Charlie Newlands

Crooked Publishing

Copyright © [2015] [Charlie Newlands]

The moral right of the author has been asserted.

All rights reserved.

No part of this publication may be reproduced, stored in a retrieval system, or transmitted, in any form or by any means, without the prior permission in writing of the publisher, nor be otherwise circulated in any form of binding or cover other than that in which it is published and without a similar condition including this condition being imposed on the subsequent purchaser.

Published by Crooked Publishing

ISBN: 978-1-5089-9606-4

Typesetting services by BOOKOW.COM

Actuality is a bitch whose wrath knows no limits. Still, we amble onward, lost forever and a day in her infinite rose garden.

For Thomas

Acknowledgments

Editing: BubbleCow / darkHouse Multimedia / Book cover design & web design: darkHouse Multimedia

CLARIFICATION & DISCLAIMER

Just to clarify, this book is a work of fiction. All characters appearing in this work are fictitious. Any resemblance to real persons, living, dead, or in a state of limbo, trapped in some weird afterlife awaiting karmic assessment and corporeal reassignment, is purely coincidental.

Contents

EViL BreW	1
Thurso and the 1980s	15
No, I'm Not Fucking Alright, Alright?!	30
Freaks and Loners	43
Run, My little One, Run!	50
The Power of Pussycats	51
Isaac's Birthday Present	55
Three Emissaries!	62
Giant Brown Slug!	63
The Poacher's Inn	92
Drugs and Aliens	110
Who the fuck is Alan Watts?	117
Wabbits	124
Spit the Blood - Cast the Spell!	141
Daffy Duck Kicked Your Arse!	142
The Ghost of Dowpy Duncan	152
Maggot Brain . . .	167

CONTENTS

Bursting the Bubble	168
Catching Flies	175
Running into the Darkness	179
Down the Bunny Hole . . .	194

EVIL BREW

The door slammed, waking me up with a jolt. A few seconds later I heard the sound of a car manoeuvring cautiously away. I could tell it had been snowing overnight, from the crunching sound of snow being compressed beneath the car's wheels. Opening one eye, I saw the beam of the taxi's headlights dart across the bedroom wall; she was gone.

Alison was heading off into the icy cold to catch the early coach from Thurso to Inverness; nearly four hours of travelling just to get to a poxy business meeting. *On a Saturday.* Later, she'd stay overnight in some grandiose hotel with her pretentious work colleagues, so they could be ready for an inevitably futile team training session the next day. *She must be crazy going all that way and missing her whole weekend for that.* My internal ranting had started, but I didn't want to engage with it. Things weren't right with us and I knew it. She was nipping at me for this and nipping at me for that, and I don't mind admitting that she was really getting on my nerves with her constant fretting about her stupid job and promotion.

Not even a simple goodbye, I thought, as I lay there in the darkness feeling hurt and increasingly wide awake. After a few failed attempts to go back to sleep I gave up on the idea and switched on the bedside lamp, sitting myself up in the bed. I reached over for yesterday's newspaper; anything to change the channel and stop myself getting worked up yet again about the state of our fading relationship. I hated all the back-biting. I never wanted any conversation to end up that way, but lately, pretty much all of them had. I let out a massive yawn as I scanned the front-page headline: **More grisly pet murders! Another gruesome trail of death is discovered as decapitated rabbits are found in gardens all over Thurso. Pet-owners demand answers after police confirm that a heavy-bladed instrument, most likely a hatchet or an axe, was used in all thirteen cases. But why would anyone do such a thing? And where are the heads?**

"Jeez," I said out loud, shaking my head. Then the doorbell rang. *Who could that be?* I asked myself, then I realised who it must be and shoved the paper and bedclothes aside and stumbled out to answer the door.

Jerry was stood there, he'd shown up early again, to come and hang out at my place for the day. This was perfectly normal, and he would often doss at my house for several days at a time. I didn't mind, I liked having him around even if Alison wasn't so keen, but it pissed me off that he would insist on showing up so early in the morning. Still, I never really had the heart to show my frustration at having to get out of my warm bed at silly o'clock for the daft bugger. During the short time that I'd known him we'd had some wicked laughs together and had become really close pals. He was funny, always making me laugh out loud and never taking himself too seriously.

He loved surfing and skateboarding, and these two pastimes were all he seemed to live for, despite the fact that he had once worked as a professional tennis coach, and was, among other things, a classically trained flautist with a Grade

EViL BreW

6 in music. Every now and again, when having a wee drinking session and a toot on the bong, he would play a bit of flute, producing the most wonderful music effortlessly, while I lay back stoned, drunk and awestruck. Happy times.

Jerry was from down south, somewhere near the city of Oxford, and had been brought up in a wealthier, higher-class setting than me, attending a private school for boys. His real name was Jeremy, but he hated it, so we generally called him Jerry or Radgie-boy, which is an endearing Scottish term for someone who is a bit kooky.

Sometimes, for a laugh, I'd put on a posh English accent and address him as Jeremy, much to his disgust. In spite of his well-to-do upbringing, it was difficult to see him as being upper class, since he lived in his van in what seemed to be abject poverty. Nevertheless, he always managed to get by without any need for a job or social security benefits, so I always assumed he had money stashed away somewhere. Not that it was any of my business of course.

Jerry just liked drifting around, looking for good waves to ride, which is why he ended up hanging around Thurso; he loved the wild surf and the eerie solitude that Caithness offered. Also, Thurso has some huge hills to skate, along with the half-pipe ramp that I ran. The ramp was housed inside an old railway shed, where trains were once fixed up, back in the day. Although the shed was part of the railway station, it was no longer in use, which meant I could rent it for very little, as an enterprising small business funded by a Prince's Trust loan.

It wasn't much to look at, but it was a place for the skaters to hang out, and running it kept me off of benefits and meant I could be my own boss. I only ever made a measly wage out of it, which barely got me by, but I was cool with that.

Anyway, the ramp was how I'd met Jerry; he was an awesome skater and would fearlessly rip the hell out of it with a death-defying precision that was a joy to watch.

Jerry had his reasons for living the life of a drifter. He had lost his wife to cancer within the short space of a year. Telling me about this was the one and only time he ever opened up about his past, his guard probably lowered by the rather large amount of whiskey we had both downed on that particular night. Whiskey can make people a wee bit emotional at times, if you know what I mean? Anyway, I didn't get the whole story, but I certainly didn't want to press the poor chap on the matter. It was clear to see the sorrow and grief welling up through the bottom of his glass.

All I know is that after he had watched his young wife go through a quick but awful descent into death, he'd had a massive breakdown that totally changed him. He walked out of his well-paid job as a tennis coach, sold his house and all his wife's personal belongings, bought a surfboard and headed out to the coast. This was all I really knew about him. So, it seemed we'd both had our lives turned upside-down by the big C, although fortunately I had survived my little battle with childhood leukaemia. I guess I was the lucky one.

Ach, the truth is, neither of us were too fussed about dwelling on all that dark shit. I liked him because he was cool and his subdued charisma was infectious, akin to that of the character that Steve McQueen played in the movie *The Great Escape*, although to look at, he was more of a dead ringer for a young Peter O'Toole in *Lawrence of Arabia*. Women were constantly falling at Jerry's feet, but this just seemed to rile him up, as though he couldn't be arsed with the attention. He was totally unassuming, yet kind of eccentric with it. He picked up women when it suited him, but it was easy to see his heart wasn't in it.

I suspected he was quietly grieving and processing, maintaining a kind of distant composure, doing his best to deal with the heartache in his own private way. Or maybe he was simply trying to forget about the whole thing and move on, preferring not to get too attached, or too deeply under the surface of things. Maybe skating and surfing were pretty apt pursuits in that case. Either way, I wasn't up for badgering him about it, I was just happy to be his pal and have a laugh.

Anyhow, on this particularly cold morning, after quickly getting dressed and wandering through to the kitchen to make some tea, I reached up for an old shoebox from the top shelf, then wandered over and sat across from Jerry, placing the box down on the coffee table. Cautiously, I removed the lid to reveal thousands of perfectly dried magic mushrooms that we had both picked from up on the golf course two months earlier. The golf course was without doubt the best place to get magic mushrooms; Jerry had a theory that you could tell when the mushrooms were going to pop up by the amount of rabbit droppings you could spot on the putting greens. Where there was lots of rabbit shit is where the magic mushrooms would grow best.

Exchanging devilish grins, we gawked for a moment at the mass of withered shrooms, having decided that today would be the day we'd brew up a mind-bending black tea from about nine hundred of them. There was clear purpose in our madness though, as we were off to an amazing event that night at the Bay Inn Hotel, a solo performance by the one and only psychedelic suzerain, Peggy Pope!

We figured that by the time of the gig we would be floating on a fluffy cloud, while enjoying a few pints of chilled lager.

I'm not sure how we came to the conclusion that a nine hundred-strong brew was a good idea, but at the time, it seemed like a good number, keeping in mind that some of our other pals were also going to show up and get smashed before the gig, and would most probably want to indulge in a cuppa or three themselves.

Jerry had that impish look in his eyes, daring me to take up the challenge. Recklessly, I did, even though, if I'm honest, I was getting pretty anxious about the whole thing, as I'd never taken a brew of that kind of strength before. Jerry assured me that I would be fine, but I knew he was different; he had no fear and seemed to operate on some other level that was a bit of a mystery to me. I had the fear of getting The Fear, as it was known. But Jerry didn't seem to care about consequences much. He jumped into situations without a second thought, always landing on his feet somehow, without any apparent effort. Still, by any measure, what we did that morning was beyond stupidity.

After bubbling up the brew in a large soup pan we both drank about five cups of the vile black concoction, we both started feeling the intense effects of the psilocin kicking in, like a slow-motion blow to the kidneys. I soon began to panic, rapidly regretting my decision to partake, which of course made me panic even more. The effects of the tea started sweeping me away like a giant wave, and I felt like I was going to lose control completely, and very quickly.

Jerry could see the shape I was getting into, rushing headlong toward meltdown, and so a decision was promptly made to get out of the house and go for a walk in the fresh morning air, along the coastal path that was nearby. It's a well-known fact that the best course of action when The Fear kicks in is to go for a walk and do everything humanly possible to change the subject.

Scuffing about in the hallway, coming up like a bag of kittens, the pair of us burst into ridiculous fits of manic cackles, while at the same time being fraught with the struggle of trying to get our shit together in a virtual, cartoon world, that only an hour earlier had felt so very, very normal. Drooling like a pair of frantic hyenas, we attempted to dress appropriately for the outdoors. I tried to put my coat on, at first inside out, then outside in, and not once, not twice, but three times. This confused the hell out of me and took an age to sort, while Jerry was laughing so much he looked like he was about to have a stroke.

Suddenly conscious of the racket we were making, my mood changed again in an instant, and I started to worry that my neighbours were overhearing our hysterics, most probably pressing their nosy bastard cups up against the wall, trying to listen in while their horrible, pinched faces frowned with disdain. Those snooping wankers were always trying to catch me out. I felt deeply troubled by this vision as I tussled with my coat some more until I finally got the damn thing on. Zipping up and stepping out of the front door, I couldn't help looking to see if any curtains were twitching, but thankfully this time there was no sign of surveillance. After we were both out and I'd locked up, I sneakily checked again just to be sure, nothing. *Good*, I thought. The coast was clear.

We trudged out into the sub-zero air while a peculiar sort of heaviness began to develop inside of me, a sensation that felt like a combination of needing a shit while being taken over by a powerful demonic force. It's hard to put into words, but all I know is, I felt confident one moment then panic-stricken the next, when it seemed like something was trying to escape from within, something that wasn't me. I desperately tried to think about less disturbing things, but my internal organs throbbed with a rush of poisonous trepidation, and it felt like my brain was dissolving into a semi-liquid gloop.

As I stumbled along, the frigid air was unconsciously sucked into my lungs, freezing them with icy needles, and making me labour harder and harder for each breath. Despite the biting cold, feelings of being slowly suffocated from within were creating an urge to tear all my clothes off and sprint ahead, while beating my chest screaming out *UG, UG, UG*, like some wild Neolithic caveman being chased by a swarm of invisible wasps. This urge was very nearly overwhelming, but of course, giving into it would have been a really daft thing to do, as the biggest snowflakes I think I have ever seen were beginning to fall all around me. The snowflakes were absurdly fluffy and huge, and it was like an overdone scene from a fantasy movie.

I suddenly felt like I was in Narnia, even though the increasingly marginalised voice of common sense in my addled mind was screaming at me to get a grip of myself. But I just couldn't deny it; it did feel like Narnia, it really did, which was wonderfully weird and funny, but also rather worrying. As we wove our way out toward the sea, my head struggled to cope with the onslaught of sensations that spun around and around and seemed to put me in a perpetual state of déjà vu. Time was becoming fluid, thoughts looping and scenes repeating themselves.

The thickening snow was helping out with the general disorientation and there were more and more moments where I wasn't sure where I was or when I was, or how long I'd been there. I started to feel like I might disappear into the swirling snow and come apart into flakes myself, spiralling away into little shreds of nothingness. I battled to keep it together, with the increasingly agonizing fear that this time we had gone too far and taken way too much, and that there would be no way back. However, there was no antidote available, and nothing to do except to keep wandering out in the snow, hoping that it would level out soon. I tried to comfort myself with the thought that at least in this weather; nobody would be around to see us acting crazy out here.

Of course, as soon as I'd had that thought, the silhouettes of a hunched, tall man and his dog materialised ahead. They seemed to be walking right towards us. "Bloody typical!" I muttered to myself. My inner voice of reason tried to reassure me that I was plain old Danny Texas, a normal human being, just out for an innocent walk with my pal, who happened to be a wee bit drunk.

However, things got rapidly worse when the figure drew closer and it became clear that it was in fact Robbie Buck, my uncle. "Holy shit!" I hissed under my breath as the sense of needing a dump redoubled its intensity in my bowels. *Stay calm and don't panic! Deny, deny, deny!* I repeated inwardly, while my teeth chattered and I clenched my fists inside the pockets of my coat. Uncle Robbie recognised me straight away, and came stomping over.

"Hello there, Danny, what are you doing out here?"

"Um, um just taking a bit of a walk, Robbie," I replied, desperately trying not to make any direct eye contact with the unwelcome fucker, knowing my pupils were probably looking like huge black marbles by now. Uncle Robbie stopped and observed me in a dubious manner. I could tell he was trying to work out what was up with me; he was such a nosy old bastard. My movements felt twitchy as anxiety oozed from every fibre of my being. I couldn't think of anything to say.

"How's your father, is he still working over the water?" he grunted at me in his deeply masculine tone of voice. By this time my heart was beating like a barn door in a force nine gale. Every word that came out of my uncle's mouth was apparently being secretly translated to me by a creepy gang of interpreters, gibbering like some woozy choir in a weird slap-back echo chamber inside my skull. My uncle asked the same old stupid question every time I banged into the nosy old twat, and irritation flashed through me as his fat, rosy-cheeked face smirked, transforming briefly into that of a cartoon gargoyle with long whiskers and pointed ears.

"Yeah, yeah, Dad's still over in Orkney." My voice squeaked with the strain of my attempt to act like I was in my right mind, which I clearly wasn't. Robbie raised an eyebrow at me and quietly asked,

"What's up with him?" For a moment I was totally confused, then I followed my uncle's gaze over towards Jerry who was several yards away, standing with his arms swinging in front of him like the pendulum of a clock. Robbie's German Shepherd had its nose firmly embedded into Jerry's crotch, and was wagging its tale energetically.

"Och, he's a bit pished up after a heavy session from last night. I was taking him out to get him some fresh air," I explained, trying to sound nonchalant but sounding strained and uptight. I hoped he'd think I was just cold. I hoped he'd think Jerry's mad pendulum impression was a way of trying to keep warm. I tried clapping my hands around my upper arms to reinforce the idea but after a few claps I realised my hands seemed to be turning into seagull's wings. I stopped doing that, and just stood there.

The snow kept falling. Jerry kept swinging. My uncle looked at us both in turn, eyebrow still raised, a quizzical expression on what seemed to me to be his increasingly grotesque, ugly face. There was an awkward silence while he considered his next move. As I stared back at Uncle Robbie, his left eye started to morph until it became three times larger than the right. It drilled into me, penetrating my flimsy façade of sobriety. His head swelled and started to look like a giant turnip, then gradually more like a gargoyle again. This pause in the conversation seemed to stretch out into eternity. I was reaching the point of screaming out in terror at the spectacle of his monstrous head, and legging it off home, but thankfully, I somehow managed to hold my nerve. Eventually, Robbie spoke again. "Right, I'll leave you boys to it," he grunted at me, then he hollered to his dog to get away from Jerry's crotch. The booming of his voice made me flinch. Then he stomped off into the blizzard, shaking his head to himself.

Jerry stood there in the falling snow with both arms still counting out some rhythm that only he could perceive. Watching my uncle disappear off into the distance, I felt an unfamiliar fear gathering within me. Had I just been interrogated by a squint-eyed gargoyle neep-man who was really an imposter pretending to be my uncle? I pondered for a moment on what possible motive the imposter might have, then shouted over to Jerry, "Oi, ya dunderheid, let's get off home, I'm losing the fucking plot here. Stop swinging your arms like that, ya crazy man!" Jerry looked up and gave me that spacey funny-cunt smile of his, acting as if nothing had happened. He was a right radge like that. We turned our faces back into the snowstorm, as the north wind whipped around us mercilessly, and headed back the way we'd come.

Once we were back at the house I found myself to be in a right flap. Annoyingly, Jerry seemed to be holding it together. I could tell this was going to be an epic trip and frankly I was still very worried. Nevertheless, there was the faint hope that things would level out; experience had taught me that if I could sit down for a bit and allow the trip to peak, then hopefully I could float downstream from there. I might even enjoy it later. I kept trying to remind myself of this while I twitched and fidgeted and tried not to look at anything for too long, as everything seemed to want to turn into something weird or disturbing.

Jerry sat there with a self-satisfied grin on his face, unfazed by all the visual palaver that kept unfolding before us. Weakly, I tried to emulate his apparent calm, but everything in my field of vision was going crazy and there was no sign of any let-up. There was no fixed point I could focus on, no anchor I could drop into reality, and little I could do to abate my sense of dread at the thought that we may indeed have ingested a suicidal dose of mushroom tea.

Feeling parched, I got up and poured myself a mug of water, which I don't mind admitting was a bit of a struggle; trying to coordinate my movements was like trying to walk across one of those inflatable bouncy castles that kids play on. Each step felt wonky and wrong. Hurriedly, I sat myself back down, feeling totally out of it.

I took a few sips from my Manchester United mug, then a few more, then a few more, but it was no good. Every sip of water crunched and popped like fine, semi-liquefied beads of glass. At first I thought that maybe I had broken a tooth or something, but for some reason, my warped mind was sure this couldn't have happened. Why? Well, because I had someone else's teeth in my mouth, of course. It must have been glass then, after all, but how had glass gotten into the drinking water?

My mind struggled for answers but only came up with more questions. Then it dawned on me that I'd just reassured myself that I had a mouth full of someone else's teeth! What the hell was that about? My brain raced on as I kept trying to drink the alarmingly crunchy glass-water. I was determined to stay calm though. Even if it drove me toward lunacy, I had to STAY CALM!

But that was becoming tough to do, as I found myself wondering if you could go permanently insane from too much mushroom tea. The question of my sanity scared me, and my fingers dug into the cushion I was sitting on. I picked up my mug again and took another look inside; it looked like murky bog water, but then I realised that it was only the bottom of the mug I was seeing. I drank from it once more. It was still crispy glass. I gazed over at Jerry who was chuckling away to himself, gawping at the television. It wasn't even switched on! *Nice lad, bit daft though*, I thought, feeling a mirthless smile stretch across my unhappy face.

My head swung back, and I closed my eyes. I immediately had a vision of the blood forcing through my veins, like some crimson-stained nightmare. I felt like it was going to suck me in and drown me, drown me in my own life-force. The bizarre, dizzying feeling was overwhelming and terrifying. Snapping out of it with a shudder and gripping my mug until my fingers went white, I looked back over at Jerry again. He was still chuckling away to himself like a mad man, still staring at the blank TV screen. I laughed out loud for a moment; a harsh, disembodied sound. Then I fell back into my woozy stupor once again, my body becoming a large lump of jelly vibrating with indecision upon a plastic plate of unreality, waiting for the bats to dissipate into monkey vapours. Then oddly, an unprompted sense of regressing back to my childhood memories took hold of me. I was gone.

Thurso and the 1980s

As I remember it, like most isolated seaside towns during the winter months, Thurso was a bit boring. In fact, dare I say it, a bit shit. And yet, I can't deny that Thurso had a certain magnetism that could keep you hanging in there through the endless cold, snow, gales and rain. The place has a strong sense of history, stretching way back to the time of the Norse Orcadians.

One good thing about the long winters, back then in the early 1980s, was that we kids got days, sometimes even weeks off from school due to the frequent, severe blizzards that swept across the county of Caithness. The temperatures would regularly plummet to ten below zero and beyond. On cold, clear nights we would often be treated to amazing displays of the Aurora Borealis, a phenomenon that had the power to draw the kids on our housing scheme away from their warm fires, television sets, radios and record players and out into the freezing darkness. We would all gather to sit on the wall by the swings in the park, away from the depressing orange glare of the street lamps, staring up at the luminous waves that rippled across the cold heavens in an awe-inspiring display of nature's power and magnificence. Yeah, Thurso certainly had its moments.

I'll bet you're asking yourself where the hell Thurso is, right? Well, it's the northernmost town in the UK, and probably one of the coldest, too. If there was an annual 'Town Most Likely To Freeze Your Bollocks Off' competition in Scotland, I reckon Thurso would have a few trophies on the shelf. Through the winter it's mostly ice and snow, and in the summer it generally blows a gale or rains, usually both. Don't get me wrong now; we did have fun in the snow, riding on the backend of shovels and plastic bin liners, whooshing down steep hills on black ice at high speed, veering wildly off course to crash into a heap of other kids who had also ended up in the middle of the main road. It didn't matter though, as we knew it was way too slippery for cars to be out, and anyway we always had someone keeping a look out for traffic.

Then there were the snowball wars with the Dooley boys who always played too rough. There was always some sort of near-fatal injury, since they played to kill, rather than merely to win. This often ended up in a dispute that led to violence. The Dooley clan were our neighbours, a band of outcasts who were generally seen as troublemakers within the town. Personally, I always liked the Dooley boys and found them to be a charming bunch of dudes, once you got to know them. They simply stuck up for each other. They were a team. A team with fists. And hard boots.

The fact that my brother and I were both born in Kettering, Northants, and had lived in Corby until I was seven years old, made life especially hard for us in Thurso. Having English accents, being relatively well-dressed and bringing with us our 'funny ways' made us an easy target with the local kids. Moving from the middle of England to the northernmost edge of Scotland was a pretty big culture shock for us too, of course.

I guess I was the luckier sibling when it came to integrating with the locals, because I quickly lost my English accent, while my brother was stuck with his Northants twang. He was eleven when we moved up north, and was forever being taunted for being English, even though the circumstances of our birth could have been seen as a small 'blip' in our lineage, since there isn't any English blood in our family history; our mum is Irish and our dad's a Scot. Not that there is anything wrong with being English, mind you, but it's a sad fact that the Scottish kids didn't look too fondly on their southern neighbours. At least, that was the case when I was at school back in the 1980s. Things have moved on a bit since then.

So yeah, my brother had to put up with being ridiculed for being the posh English boy at school, even though we weren't posh; far from it! He stuck up for himself though, and the class hard-nuts soon backed off when they realised what a psycho he could be when pushed. He was like a box of fireworks when he lost his temper, pretty scary, but in a freaky, psychotic way. He was always a bit of a black sheep, my brother; forever straying off into his own world of solitude, avoiding everybody as much as possible. He was a strange one, alright.

Yeah, life could be harsh back then. When the snow eventually melted, it turned to a drab, gritty sludge that seemed to linger for much longer than it should have done. We would have to endure long months of hibernation, sitting indoors, shivering around a crappy three-bar electric fire, which was the only source of heat in Mum and Dad's freezing cold council house. You could hear the north wind howling outside, while my old man would be upstairs playing his irritating Scottish folk music on a button-key accordion, wheezing out the same set of songs over and over again.

The 1980s were arguably the weirdest period in my life; at least that's how it feels when I look back at it. Dad could never hold down a job, not that there were any jobs to hold down. We were skint. Everyone was skint. It was the Thatcher era; a time of mass unemployment, the often violent and bloody clashes at the miners' strikes, and the infamous Brighton Hotel bombings, carried out by the Provisional Irish Republican Army. Confrontation and revolt were in the air!

There were times when I would watch my old man sitting there on his usual chair, a pot-bellied Elvis look-alike, filling the room with toxic smoke as he chuffed away obliviously on one of his smelly fags, tut-tutting at the BBC news on the telly while pretending to himself that he had some sort of deep intellectual grasp of it all. Heh! Yeah, like fuck.

All he ever really did back in those days was spend his time being a grumpy bastard, moaning about this, moaning about that, or else moaning at Mum to go to the pub with him. She'd often snarl back at him through clenched teeth that, "There's no money for pubs! There's scarcely any fecken money for food!" He didn't care though. The pub was all he lived for in those days, it being his only escape from the doldrums and the only thing that stopped his moaning. So, as you can imagine, we never saw that much of him, and when we did, he was mostly hung-over, oblivious to the fact that he had two sons. Mum would always defend him, reminding us that he was incapable of showing love towards us because he'd never been loved himself, like that was somehow supposed to make us feel better . . .

Fair play to him though, there was always bread on the table and milk in the fridge. He always found a way to make a penny. He was very old-fashioned and had typical working class values, along with the obligatory chip on his shoulder; everyone was looking down their nose at him, but of course it never dawned on him that he might be the one with the snobbery problem.

His grandparents had brought him up, because his father was over in France fighting the Nazis in the Second World War and his mother was a dysfunctional alcoholic at the time. She struggled to cope with a baby and her seven other children who were subsequently being looked after by relatives so she could get on with doing what she did best; getting blind drunk. She was a bit wild by all accounts; four feet high and hard as fuck, with a metal pole in her leg, which made her walk funny. Apparently, she'd fallen out of a parked aeroplane while pished out of her skull and shattered her leg on the concrete. What the hell she was doing drunk in a parked aeroplane, I have no idea.

There was another rumour going about that she'd had an affair with an Italian prisoner of war over in the Orkneys and that my dad had been the direct result of this romantic fling. He looked a bit Italian, right enough, although he always played down any tittle-tattle about the subject. He would have none of it, seeing himself as a true, proud Scot, who foolishly ran off to London when he was a young man 'to try and make a *penny*' as he would always put it.

He mainly worked as a concrete finisher on building sites and this is where he brewed up his hatred of city life. He would rant on at us all about his disgust for London and Englanders. Nevertheless, he stayed there for a good five years, dating a Jamaican woman who couldn't understand a word he said but somehow found his Scottish/Italian charisma funny and endearing. Of course, this all ended in tears when she ran off with a Welsh guy who was supposed to be Dad's best mate. So the rumour goes anyway, according to our mum.

After that he got a job at the steel works in Corby, driving trucks and diggers. At one time, the town was known locally as 'Little Scotland' because of the large influx of Scottish migrant workers who'd moved there. That's where he met my mum, on a night out at the Irish club. She had moved to Corby from London to make a go of it in this modern town of opportunity, and to be nearer her married sister who had moved there some time earlier. It was her sister who got her a job working in a crisp factory.

Mum originally came from a place called, 'Newcastle West' or 'An Caisleán Nua Thiar' in Irish, which is a town in the west of County Limerick in Ireland. Her father was a pig farmer and a part-time member of the IRA, back in the day. He was also a notorious drunkard and a tight-fisted wife-beater, by all accounts. My mum had to have him shipped over from Ireland, kicking and screaming, to our old house in Corby when he was too old and frail to look after himself properly. Sadly, he outlived his long-suffering wife by about five years, but he couldn't cope on his own without her. So when his eldest daughter (my Aunty May) moved out of the farmhouse to come across the Irish Sea and be with her two other sisters, he had to come too. It was messy, and no one was very happy about the situation.

It would seem that this belligerent old Irishman was reaping what he'd sown though; there was little love for him, and his now adult daughters were none too keen to have him turn up in their lives again, like the proverbial bad penny. In tandem with their displeasure, my dad was spitting sparks at the idea of having an old IRA veteran living in his house. So, nobody was really rolling out the red carpet.

My brother can vaguely remember our Irish granddad, but I can't because I was only about two years old at the time. Mum told me about it when I was older. The story goes that after a few weeks of being stuck indoors, with Mum and Dad doing alternate shifts in their factory jobs, the old Irishman got a severe case of cabin fever, and unexpectedly vanished out of the back door one sunny morning. Mum, true to form, panicked and contacted the police, who put a missing persons search out for him. Search teams wandered the fields and industrial wasteland at the back of our street, thinking that he may have lost the plot and wandered off into the undergrowth.

Two days later, after much worry, the old boy was found in the cellar of the local pub, *The Raven*, where it was assumed he must have tumbled drunkenly down the cellar steps, thinking it was the way to the gents. Nobody had seen this happen, and the barman had unwittingly shut the cellar doors some time later, unintentionally locking him in. He was discovered sprawled out in his own faeces, pished as a fart, having helped himself to a fair selection of the pub's finest malts. This was perhaps understandable, since he'd suffered two broken legs and a fractured hip during the fall.

He was eventually brought to the hospital after he had tried to behead one of the ambulance men with his walking stick, while singing Irish freedom songs at the top of his voice. Shortly after arriving, he upped and died. Mum reckoned he was too pished to know much about it, so at least he went out fairly painlessly, merrily fighting the oppressors 'til the bitter end, just the way he would have wanted it. As a saving grace, his corpse was sent back to Ireland where he was finally laid to rest.

The story goes that the night before his funeral, my mother and her other sisters all witnessed that old Celtic spectre, *the banshee,* wailing and flailing around outside the upstairs windows of the old farmhouse where they had all been brought up and where they were supposed to be staying. Of course, they all took off in a fit of wild terror and spent the night at a neighbour's house, three miles away. Apparently, the banshee followed as they ran from the house, floating along above the ditch at the side of the road, scaring the bejesus out of them. Hah!

I never really believed the story, but I will say that I was always somewhat impressed and disturbed by the terrified look in my mother's eyes whenever she recalled that fateful night. Adding to the eeriness of the tale, her sisters always backed up every word, telling it exactly the same way. So although I was sceptical, I'll admit to having had a few goose bumps on hearing that story recounted over the years, mostly because it was as though Mum was, well, telling the truth . . . It has to be pointed out here though, that my mum's lot were equally as odd as my dad's family, except that they were educated and deeply religious, but yeah, just as messed up in their own way.

Now, my brother Karl didn't get on with Dad at all. In fact, to put it plainly, they hated each other. Whenever they were in a room together the constant bickering would drive Mum and me out of the door, rolling our eyes. These arguments would sometimes turn into full-on punch-ups. Karl never really forgave Dad for some of the brutality he'd had dished out to him as a boy, and as soon as he was big enough to hit back, he would readily respond in kind, given enough provocation.

Karl seemed to have this uncanny talent for pressing all of Dad's buttons at once. A good example is the time when we were on holiday, camping on the west coast of Scotland with our aunt and two cousins from Corby. Karl was about thirteen at the time, when cousin Gordon, who was about the same age, made the unwise decision to tease Karl for liking punk rock and for being a secret fan of Adam and the Ants, a band who were, in Gordon's eyes, a bunch of poofs in girly pirate make up. Gordon had kept up his little teasing campaign throughout the day until Karl finally snapped.

True to form, Karl had flown into one of his blind rages, and in a moment of utter lunacy decided to push Gordon off the side of the steep hill that we'd climbed up. We'd been sent up there by our parents to try to escape from the swarms of midges below, where my dad was foolishly setting up camp. When I say steep hill, it was more of a cliff edge to tell the truth; not a sheer drop, but steep enough to kill a falling person should their descent gather any kind of momentum.

I watched on with my other cousin, James, both of us speechless, as Gordon tumbled and bounced through a sea of spiky purple heather and thorny yellow gorse until he eventually disappeared from view, his futile screams for help growing fainter and fainter. As Gordon disappeared in a distant puff of dust and twigs, we looked back at Karl who just stood there with a homicidal glint in his eyes, clucking to himself in a menacing fashion, bold as brass and guilty as fuck.

Turning our gaze toward the camp, we could see the adults taking a moment to comprehend what had just happened, the seconds ticking past in slow motion while Gordon failed to reappear on the skyline, their eyes then turning to us. James ran down towards them, to grass up Karl; James was a right snitch. He needn't have bothered though, because the adults had witnessed for themselves exactly what Karl had just done.

Gordon failed to reappear, slowly their faces contorted in horror and panic, as it dawned on them that they might have just witnessed a murder. Dad was already in a shitty mood after many failed attempts at putting up a six-man tent in a persistent cloud of midges, while burning up in the blazing hot sunshine.

As you can no doubt imagine, he went absolutely fucking ballistic. His initial reaction was to sprint as fast as he could, up the hill and after my now terrified older brother, eventually catching him and attempting to lay into him with his leather belt. Luckily for Karl, Dad's belt got stuck in his bunched up belt loops, making him look like a right twat as he yanked and swore at his own trousers, until in a white-hot fury he grabbed my brother by the scruff of the neck and marched him back down the hill, all the while man-slapping him around the back of the head before, weirdly, picking him up by his jacket and throwing him in the boot of his car, which he slammed shut and locked!

That first important business taken care of, a look of real worry then passed over his face as he started to realise that our cousin was probably at the very least seriously injured, if not fully dead. There was an odd hiatus then, as everyone looked on in dread while Dad scrambled back up the hill and then clambered gingerly down the cliff face to try to find and rescue Gordon. When he eventually reappeared with the lad, to everyone's absolute amazement it seemed he'd only suffered a few cuts and bruises, although he was clearly in a state of shock and trembling visibly.

Perhaps unsurprisingly, Karl has suffered from severe claustrophobia and anxiety attacks ever since being locked in the boot of Dad's car on that ill-fated day. He still goes into irrational, sweaty panics in small or crowded places. He tries to play down his phobia, but I know for a fact that although he avoided the belt that day, he didn't escape the experience unscathed.

Another incident I remember was when Dad, in a blind fit of rage, beat the crap out of Karl with a plastic hose, a weapon of opportunity that was normally attached to the vacuum cleaner. This particular whupping was for getting into trouble with the law and making a name for himself in the local newspaper as a thief and a vandal, thereby bringing terrible shame upon the family. Karl was dressing more and more like a punk rocker, and Dad was clearly agitated and sickened by this rebellious punk phase, which was obviously to blame for him deciding to have a wee go at law breaking.

His first try at crime was to break into the high school's tuck shop with his two pals, Wee Alf and Big Jim. I'm not sure if they had planned in advance to do this dreadful deed or if it was just a spontaneous moment of adolescent foolishness, but between them they stole about two hundred quid's worth of chocolate and crisps. This booty was of course sold on to all the other kids from the housing scheme over the next few weeks.

However, for some stupid reason they broke into the school again, only this time they vandalised a classroom and set fire to a wastepaper bin in the hope it would burn down the school. Sadly, all it did was set off the fire alarms, scaring Karl and his pals away. Fortunately for them, the plastic bin just melted into a lump of gunk and the fire went out.

Mum nearly divorced Dad over the aftermath of that little incident. Karl was so black and blue after his beating from the old man that Mum decided to put some space between them both by sending Karl down to Corby for a few weeks over the summer holidays, to spend time with our English cousins. The truth is that Mum was too ashamed to let Karl be spotted by our nosey, blethering neighbours, and dare I say, a little nervous that more serious questions would be asked about the extreme violence that had been inflicted on him.

Sending my brother to Corby to cool off for the summer didn't do any good though; in fact it made things worse because he started hanging around with our less than virtuous cousin Gordon. This did seem a bit odd, considering their antagonistic history and the 'cliff face incident', but for some reason Gordon forgave my brother. At that time, Gordon was becoming a bit of a handful for his stressed-out mother. She had gone through a divorce and was doing her best to cope with her two teenage boys on her own, while living on a single wage.

Karl and Gordon had themselves been hanging around with a kid called Freddy, whose dad had just got out of the clink, having done time for aggravated burglary and attempted murder. Apparently, Freddy's dad had taught him a clever trick (one among many others) that he had picked up while doing his stretch, the trick being a rather ingenious way to swindle cash from fruit machines.

Basically, you wrapped electrical tape around the edge of a ten pence piece five times, and then carefully trimmed the excess tape off with a razor blade, thereby making the ten pence piece equal in weight and circumference to a fifty pence piece. Then, when you stuck one of these pimped up coins into a ten pence-per-go fruit machine, it would either give you a game and forty pence change, or some of the older machines would give you five games, which upped your chance of winning the jackpot. Either way you were onto a winner, so long as you didn't get caught, that is. They were delighted when they tried it and found out that it actually worked.

So on the strength of this little scam, Freddy teamed up with Gordon and Karl and proposed a master plan that was going to make them all filthy rich. The three of them then hit every fruit machine in Corby with their counterfeit fifty pence pieces and within a week they had cashed up about three hundred quid's worth of ten pence pieces between them, at several post offices and shops around the town. In order to not look suspicious, they cashed in small amounts at a time; making out it was coinage from their piggy bank savings. They then frittered away their 'winnings' on chip butties, booze, clothes and records.

However, during one last gambling spree, they made the fateful mistake of returning to the Irish Club for the third time in a week, whereupon a doorman recognised them and challenged them about their age, suspecting they were up to no good. Our cousin got lippy, so much so that the doorman grabbed him by the scruff of the neck and there was a bit of a struggle, ending up with the carrier bag containing the dodgy coins spilling all over the floor.

Apparently, my brother and Freddy were chased around the town for a full hour until they were eventually caught by some of the bar staff and marched up to the police station, where they were all thrown into cells for the night for refusing to confirm who they were. After being interrogated for five hours, they finally confessed to the crime, each of them secretly accusing another of being the ringleader. Honour amongst thieves, eh?

Although our aunty went absolutely ape-shit at Gordon and Karl, neither Mum nor Dad ever found out about this because our aunt knew Karl would get the hiding of his life when he went back home to Scotland. She took pity on him and stayed quiet about the matter, but I reckon he should have got a good hiding for being such knob-head. Funnily enough, Karl never got into trouble with the law again after that; I think a night cooped up in a police cell scared the bejesus out of him, although he would never admit to the fact. Fecken ponce!

It wasn't all-bad though. We did play loads of football when we were teenagers, which by and large kept us out of trouble. We were football crazy! Even Karl was up for a game of footie when the mood took him. His pal Big Jim was the best goalkeeper in town; while the rest of us were all, well, crap, if I'm honest. Even so, we played a bit for *Thurso Thistle*, one of the local football clubs, albeit the most rubbish football club in the county at the time. Not once did we ever win a single game! It was good fun all the same, until it became way too competitive and fights broke out on the football pitch and referees were spat on and head-butted. But hey-hoe, that's how it goes sometimes when playing the beautiful game and emotions are running high.

Then there was the tennis craze, which mostly consisted of smacking a ball against a wall down at the high school. Occasionally we would find enough pennies to be able use the posh courts down in the town and have a proper game, but it never came to much. After that came the table tennis craze, a game with which we all became completely obsessed for a while, until again, fights broke out and we were all banished from the sports centre for smashing the place up in a mini teenage riot. Well, I did say sports *mostly* kept us out of trouble. Ah, the high spirits of youth . . .

My brother turned sixteen and became more and more of a loner, looking ever more weird with his poncey Goth hair. He even started wearing eyeliner at one point, which freaked the old man right out. Aye, he soon grew out of his wee punk phase when he started listening to pish shoe-gazing bands like Joy Division, Echo and the Bunnymen, and

The Teardrop Explodes. It made him withdraw from law-breaking and outwardly kicking against the system, which you could argue was a good thing, but then he withdrew from *everything*. He started wearing black clothes all the time, became a vegetarian and began reading books about art, philosophy and poetry.

A pretentious twat was how I saw him at the time. I mean, why did *my* big brother have to go and get into this airy-fairy, shoe-gazing bollocks? Seriously, why couldn't he just keep on being normal, like me? What was wrong with a bit of ska, eh? Fecken toss-bag. Bah!

Anyway, Dad didn't have a clue how to deal with my brother at this stage (nothing new there, I guess) and it was obvious that Karl didn't give a flying fuck what anyone thought of him. If he ever had been before, Karl was no longer interested in family matters and was looking for a way to escape from the doldrums of Thurso and run off to the bright lights of the city. At that point though, he was still at school and trying to scrape some qualifications together in the vain hope of being able to get some sort of dead-end job; one that probably only existed in the make-believe world of the Job Centre.

The subject of him leaving Thurso to run off to Glasgow or, even worse, London, became a contentious one with Mum and Dad, but mainly Dad, as he was of the opinion that Karl should never leave the county of Caithness; beyond that was only trouble and strife and the rat-race! The resistance gradually fizzled out though, and besides, Dad was becoming a bit scared of Karl, after taking a right hook on the chin that nearly knocked him out cold, over a dispute about music being played too loudly or some other bollocks.

No, I'm Not Fucking Alright, Alright?!

Some kind of telepathic signal seemed to be distracting me from my random memories of my youth. Straining to catch it, I struggled back to the present and opened my eyes slowly, then suddenly remembered that my pals were supposed to be showing up for a bit of a pish-up before the Peggy Pope gig. For a few sweet moments I felt okay, but as quickly as that pleasant sensation spread through me it was chased away, as a million more childhood memories rushed through my skull like a mob of elderly punters grabbing for bargains in the January sales.

My mind started picking over every teeny little thing, every miniscule detail, until I started to feel flustered and nauseous. It was as if it was trying to unravel something, get to the bottom of some nagging feeling that all was not well, searching for an answer to a question that I hadn't even come up with yet. This feeling of deep disquiet rapidly re-established that my brief sense of things being 'normal' was complete and utter bollocks, and I began to dread once more that there was no way I was ever going to come down from this.

I realised I was still in the grip of The Fear. *Normal, normal,* I said to myself. The word *normal* then began looping and echoing around my agitated mind like some devil-child, taunting me in a sing-song voice. *Normal, normal, what the fuck is normal?* I lay there, trying not to panic, wondering what would come next.

The doorbell rang. Without giving it a second thought, I grappled to get off the sofa and onto my feet, making for the front door. The room still felt like an inflatable bouncy castle, but what made it even stranger was that my movement took on a slow motion quality that made me feel disengaged from my body. This made me laugh out loud, unexpectedly; a judder of molten bliss rippled through my spine for a tenth of a second, yet in my mind it seemed to go on far longer than that.

My feet lifted off the ground and I levitated toward the door like a vampire. I put the key in the lock and started wriggling it about trying to get it to unlock, becoming more and more agitated until I became entirely rattled with the situation. I tried with all my might but I couldn't open the door. Stepping back, I began to wonder why I was opening this fucking door anyway; a question, which quickly changed to whose door, *is this anyway? And why do I have to be the one to open it?*

I stuck my head around the corner to see if Jerry could have a go, but it was no good; he had his back turned to me, swishing his arms, only this time at an astonishing speed. At the same time, he was watching something intently on the switched-off TV in the corner of the room. It seemed rude to disturb him.

Courageously, I decided to have one more go at it. To my surprise, the door abruptly swung open, like a cosmic star gate, and sure as fuck there they were; Tony, Fergus, Wallace and Cormag, all hunched and shivering in the falling snow.

Their carry-outs of beer and whiskey were tucked tightly under their arms, wrapped in carrier bags that flapped about annoyingly in the wind. I just stared at them, anxiety squeezing every tendril of my reasoning. Then, the strange silence was broken. "Alright, Danny boy?" Tony swayed in front of me with open arms. He was drunk and reeked of fags.

"No, I'm not fucking alright, *alright*?!" My response was short and sharp, the words leaping from my throat of their own accord. Taken aback, they all glanced at each other, jaws chattering in the cold, and then rather awkwardly they stepped past me, one by one, into the front room. They were greeted by the unsettling sight of Jerry standing in front of the blank television, laughing his tits off as tears poured down his face, still swinging his arms, but now at a slower pace. *How many hours has he been doing that for?* I wondered to myself. Truth was, I had lost all concept of time. Jerry glanced over at us all for a moment, and then waved. "Alright, boys?" he asked cheerfully, then turned back and carried on swinging his arms. He started clucking at the television again as if he were watching something really funny on it.

I couldn't help wondering how he seemed to be dealing with this massive dose of shrooms so much better than I was, even if his behaviour was a bit peculiar. *Fecken radgie-boy!* I barked inwardly at myself, feeling somewhat deflated by this. Then a sense of guilt over being so riled with my pals seeped into my heart. The poor buggers had walked through a blizzard from one end of the town to the other, simply to hang out with me. *What a selfish twat I am sometimes,* I thought. The guilt spread like treacle and I felt shamed. Tony started swaying about and laughing to himself while giving me that conspiratorial look of his. "Shut the fecken door, ya nutter!" he laughed at me. I realised I was still holding the cosmic portal open, and so I swung it closed, my attention drawn to a pile of wind-blown snow melting on the mat. I started to wonder why there was snow inside my house, but then Tony spoke again. "You two have been at them shrooms, I see, and it's only two-thirty in the afternoon, you pair of radges. I thought we were all supposed to be doing them together, ya cheeky feckers!"

"Two-thirty? Is that really the time? Jesus, where did the morning go?" I wondered out loud. The others started sniggering among themselves, rapidly making me feel as paranoid as fuck again. I let out a long, raspy sigh. Tony gave me a warm smile then slapped me hard on the back, momentarily knocking the wind out of me, the daft fanny, and then the cheeky fecker started dishing out orders to get a fresh brew on. In a kind of Pavlovian response, I wandered over to the kitchen area and lit the gas on the stove. It came on with a low thump, making me jump back for fear of getting burnt. Timidly, I picked up the wooden spoon and started stirring the jet-black brew.

Gazing into the dark liquid for longer than I probably should have done, I noticed it starting to pulsate, before transforming itself into what looked like a mass of tiny, greasy eels. I stood there in total bewilderment as their little oily tales flicked in and out of the black ink. *Shit, can mushrooms turn into tiny eels?* I wondered. I really didn't know what to do about this, but gazing over at the rest of the loons and seeing how keen they were to partake, I signalled with a nod of the head that they could help themselves to the devilish concoction.

Turning the cooker off carefully, I stepped back to make way for them. As they crowded around, I started fussing with the stove in an instinctive effort to avoid eye contact, feeling fresh guilt at my failure to inform them that not only were there in fact nine hundred shrooms stewed into the crazy, mind-bendingly and possibly lethal brew, but that a mass of tiny eels were now swishing about in it too. *Ach, they'll be all right,* I thought to myself, unconvincingly.

I watched with pure repugnance as Tony, Fergus, Wallace and Cormag all helped themselves, like dehydrated puppies, to the sickening slop. I felt myself heaving. Then I found myself wondering again how those eels came to be in my soup pan. *Maybe they came from inside the mushrooms?* I couldn't work it out.

At the same time, my brain was trying to keep one eye on what was going on around me, because secretly I was also starting to wonder who the -fuck these people were, and how come I knew all their names? *If they've come here through a cosmic portal,* I reasoned, *they could be anyone.* Here and there, in moments of clarity, I could hear my own voice reassuring me that I was going to be okay; *you're tripping out, it'll pass. Just stay calm . . . JUST STAY CALM!*

But it was no good. I was losing all sense of who I was, caught up in a big, nauseating, psychedelic wave of emotions that drove me to question things over and over again. *Who the fuck am I? Whose house is this? Who are these people?* Then, I heard my inner voice saying *drink water, you numpty, drink water!* But that was no good either, because every sip I took crunched in my mouth as though it was made of the kind of wafer-thin glass that light bulbs are made of. Adding to my misery, I was still pretty sure this was happening because I had someone else's bastard teeth in my gob!

I didn't know how long I'd been loitering around the kitchen, lost in my own troubles, but eventually I became aware of Wallace. Clearly, he was already tripping out as he haphazardly reached over and turned on the TV, all the while cackling like an escaped lunatic who had swallowed a whole bottle of happy-pills. His face was lit up like a fake Christmas tree with that bargain-basement tinsel chintz. *The brew is doing its work!* said a disembodied voice in my head, then it cackled like the evil witch in the *Wizard of Oz*. It seemed to echo up toward me from some deep, dark place below. For a brief moment a malevolent, twisted grin flicked across my face.

An episode of the *The Banana Splits* came on the TV. Everyone, except Fergus that is, started singing the theme tune. Jerry stopped swishing his arms and grabbed his flute from his bag, joining in with the music in perfect harmony. "*La la la, la la la la, la la la, la-la la-la la* . . ." everyone was chanting, like a bunch of spaced-out football fans. For a moment, I too felt the urge to be a part of what was happening, and so I ambled woozily back to the living area. God only knows what we must have looked like; a bunch of zombie-clowns dancing about in a disturbing scene from a deeply confusing nightmare, I guessed.

I tried to join in with the singing, but I couldn't get in synch, because I was becoming too distracted with the way everyone was starting to appear to me. My *la la la's* turned into a kind of hysterical laughter; not with joy from seeing my pals having a good time, no, nae chance of that! I was laughing along with a rapidly growing fear, horrified to see that they had become a bunch of singing, swaying, hideous impish-looking creatures, with whiskers. *With whiskers? Why did this keep happening?*

This was unpredictably weird and sinister as fuck and I couldn't stop staring at everyone. In fact, as I scrutinised my house, I became aware of how small and unfamiliar everything seemed, and how it was all suddenly very cartoon-like. I felt unsteady and sat down, watching a bunch of twitchy-nosed goblins slurping down black eel juice and losing their fucking minds in a tiny house that I thought might possibly have belonged to me, but I was no longer sure of anything.

My brain raced, trying desperately to work out what was *actually* going on, but the TV sucked us all in and we seemed unable to do anything but carry on watching *The Banana Splits*. It seemed to be going on forever, and despite the funny antics on screen, I began to realise that it really wasn't making me happy. Fergus didn't seem to be having much fun either, as he looked over at me with a terrified expression on his face.

Then the TV was unexpectedly turned off. I felt a moment of partial relief as my own fear level dropped down a notch, but it didn't last long. Tony had turned off the telly, deciding it was time for some 'proper' music, and had dropped some vinyl onto the turntable. Mistakenly, the daft fanny had decided it would be a really cool idea to put on *Trout Mask Replica* by Captain Beefheart.

As the needle crackled from the edge of the vinyl into the first track, I was frowning deeply, biting my lower lip. I knew what lurked inside those grooves. This was a fucking *terrible* idea as far as I was concerned, and I was sure that Tony bloody well knew it. *This is a terrible, terrible idea,* I fired at him mentally, giving him daggers, but even though a new hell was descending upon me, I was mute and immobile, transfixed by the disturbing appearance of my bewhiskered goblin-friends. *What the fuck are they doing?* I thought to myself. *Are they trying to drive me insane?*

It's always seemed to me that Captain Beefheart is a verbal prankster and that his music (especially *Trout Mask Replica*) is laced with hidden obscenities that play on your inner fears at the best of times. Most people I know agree that this particular album is full of bad voodoo and can easily fuck up the equilibrium of the most sober of listeners, and should not be approached lightly! The very idea of throwing down this particular gauntlet in these particular circumstances seemed totally nuts.

To make things worse, Jerry started swinging his arms like a pendulum again, and the sneaky fucker knew full well he was messing with my head. I looked around at the rest of my so-called pals, as they sat there like smug fuckers with their self-satisfied smirks. *So they think they can happily sit through this accursed Dadaism that poses as an album, eh? Aye, let's see how long these chumps last once the Captain messes with their heads*, I said to myself. *Let's watch Rome fucking well burn!* I clung to my seat as track two kicked in.

A sinister throb filled the room with the Captain banging on about Kleenex hanging on twigs, beans stuck in the bottom of a bowl, and some girl named Bimbo Limbo Spam. On it went, and nobody seemed to be making any move to stop it. *Jesus H. Christ, these nutters are seriously going to do this,* I thought, as I clung to my seat while the Captain yelled through the speakers at us all, tying our minds in knots with tortuous thought trails and disturbing visions. Like I needed any help with that.

Time seemed to lose its forward thrust, and I felt like I'd become trapped in some kind of eternal sonic purgatory. *Fucking hell, this is only track four! How am I going to manage sitting through another twenty-four tracks of this? Why the fuck did I even buy this album?* I recalled then that I hadn't bought it, but that it had been recommended by the DJ John Peel, so my brother, being a pretentious shoe-gazer, had rushed out and got it the next day. Thinking I was the crafty one, I'd skilfully pilfered it from him when he fucked off to Glasgow, leaving half his record collection behind. Sitting there now in aural turmoil, I guessed that this was one of those moments where karma was proving itself to be a viable concept. The only reason I even knew about Captain Beefheart was because of Karl ranting on about how amazingly unique and avant-garde he was. *Why did my brother have to be weird?* I asked myself. *I mean, what's wrong with a bit of UB40 or The Specials, eh?*

Jerry was still whupping his arms around like a crazy man, but this time with an evil smile stretched across his face that really scared me. Fergus had stopped his manic laughing now and was clinging to his seat for dear life, apparently terrified. His skin had turned a horrible shade of grey, but I didn't want to tell him about it in case it gave the poor boy The Fear. Wallace was still head-banging, but was obviously faking it now; I could tell he had hurt his neck, but was still trying to be king head-banger. To me he just looked like a bit of a prat. *Aye, rock on*, I thought, mirthlessly.

As for Tony, well, he was pretending he was 'still' reading the back of the album cover; yeah, like fuck could anyone spend that long reading an album cover! I could tell he was now suffering from a sense of hellish, claustrophobic juju, just like I was. I gave him a stare but he carried on pretending to be reading the album cover. *Aye, got you sussed, pal!*

Then out of the blue my attention switched and I became fixated with Fergus's rather disturbing assertion that *The Banana Splits* were all coming over to my house. He'd started ranting on and on about it, until I became highly agitated by the notion, unable to see how they were going to get their stupid psychedelic moon buggies into my shrinking living room. *There isn't enough space, damn it!* I sat there agonizing about the situation, unaware that I had the palms of my hands pressed against the sides of my temples and must have been looking a bit desperate. Of course, I had clocked that my pals were coming up like rockets flying out of a dead chicken's arse, so I probably should have been able to put this troubling notion into a clearer perspective, but I didn't seem to be very good at perspective any more.

A shadow blocked out the light; it was Wallace. I looked up at him for a moment as he stood over me, swaying slightly, then he sat down next to me, resting his arm on my hunched shoulders. Feeling deeply uncomfortable, I could only stare back at him as he asked me what was up.

He repeated the question about thirty-million fucking times, in slow motion, until I couldn't take it anymore and I realised I was going to have to respond. As I began to speak, I found myself breaking down with emotional stress as I tried to confess that I just couldn't see how we were going to cope with those fucking moon buggies everywhere, but I kept losing my trail of thought because of the antics of the others who were all going totally loo-la to the soundtrack of *Trout Mask* fucking *Replica*, which was still pelting out of my speakers at full whack. Resentment welled up in me. *Cunts won't be so cocky when The Banana Splits show up, eh?*

I looked back at Wallace. "I'm really *worried*, Wallace," I shouted in his ear, wild-eyed. Wallace looked at me with some genuine concern, although the close proximity of his impish characteristics was now seriously unnerving the fuck out of me too. "Worried? What are you worrying about, Danny?"

"THEM!" I yelled back, shocked that he didn't understand.

"Who?" Wallace looked baffled. "This lot?"

I snapped back; "No, you know exactly who I'm talking about! Don't act the funny-cunt wi' me, *pal*." I gave him a threatening look, as fear and anger vied for pole position in my strung-out mind. Wallace seemed perplexed and was shaking his head at me as if I had gone absolutely bonkers. "You're talking a load of dribble, my friend."

At this, I got really upset and lashed out at him. "*The Banana Splits*! That's who I'm fucking-well talking about, as if you didn't know already, ya fanny! I mean, how the fuck are they going to get those stupid buggies in here, eh?" I shrieked into his face. "They'll never fit, for fuck's sake!" The room suddenly became still and all eyes were now on me, as mind-mangling sounds kept on leaping out of the speakers like a horde of satanic baboons looking for a skull to crush.

Fergus turned the volume down, and then spoke up. "Aye, Danny's right, there's no room in here for those Banana Splits cunts and their psychedelic moon buggies; someone is going to have to step up and tell those cunts to get fucked!" The others looked at each other in open-mouthed confusion, wondering what the hell we were talking about. *Aye, playing the funny cunts too, I see*, I said to myself. I was sure they knew full well what Fergus was going on about. Doubtful about who or what to trust, I took the decision to keep my mouth shut at this point, but I was sure that something bad was coming. It was all getting way too intense and I was developing an urge to curl up into a ball and sit this shit out.

Cormag stepped in then, and quietly explained to Fergus and me that we appeared to be having a bit of a meltdown, and kindly reassured us both that there was no such thing as *The Banana Splits*; it was just a kids' TV programme from the late 1960s. Fergus looked confused for a moment, "You're not being a kidder now, is it really a 1960s kids' programme?" he asked suspiciously. Cormag reached over and gently put his hand on Fergus's shoulder. "I'm not being a kidder, mate, it really is a 1960s kids' programme. *The Banana Splits* are not real. They're not coming round with their buggies." He looked at each of us in turn, "It's alright, lads," he said, candidly.

Fergus was lost in his own thoughts for a moment and I just stared back at them both, feeling completely confused. Perhaps because of the reassuring tone of Cormag's voice, I began to come a little closer to my senses for a few brief moments, despite the fact that everyone in the room was now kind of fleecy-looking, as though they had tufty, furry bits appearing around their outlines and everything was still utterly fucking weird.

Grasping at reality, I partially convinced myself that I probably *was* just tripping out and these lads *were* actually my pals, not a bunch of increasingly fluffy, shape-shifting interlopers. A sense of lost dignity came over me. How embarrassing, to lose the plot like this in front of all my mates, and so early in the day as well. *Ach well*, I thought, *at least I'm not alone. I mean, Fergus appeared to be losing it too . . .*

The boys decided that the best thing for me to do was to go and have a wee chill-out in the bedroom, seeing as I had become a little overly emotional with it all. Fergus was told to shut up about *The Banana Splits*; it was no longer up for discussion. In other words, they wanted me to get the fuck out of the way for a bit and for Fergus to calm down. Everyone recognised that The Fear could spread like a virus; better to keep Fergus and me apart. Cormag led me out of the living room.

A meltdown, as my fellow heads would refer to it, is not a state for the faint-hearted. It was not a place I was keen on visiting either. *Thank Christ Alison's away*, I found myself thinking as I approached the bed. At least I didn't have her to worry about right now. The idea of her finding out that I had drunk the juice of nine hundred magic mushrooms that had somehow curdled into tiny eels didn't bear thinking about. She hated the idea of psychedelics, and drugs in general, and I knew for a fact she would go pure mental at the very thought of me cooking tiny eels in our soup pan. She had a serious phobia of any kind of slithery creatures.

My mind began conjuring disastrous scenarios like miniature horror movies, but then I became dimly aware again of Cormag's presence and the echoing sound of his voice, reassuring me that I just needed to rest and calm down. He switched off the light then shut the bedroom door gently. Lying on the comfortable bed and closing my eyes, I felt myself drifting backwards and downwards, as though I was being sucked into a dark lair of childhood memories.

Freaks and Loners

Without a shadow of doubt, school was a very dangerous place for a teenager to be back then. When I say, 'back then', I mean back in the early 1980s. The county of Caithness has two principal, rival towns; Thurso and Wick, the residents of which, in my experience, generally fucking hate each other.

Unluckily for me, the location of our school meant it had its doors open to kids from both of these historic burghs, with roughly a fifty-fifty mix. It was a massive school that looked like a cross between a high security prison and a rundown NHS hospital, with a few large playing fields attached to it. But then, most schools of that era looked that way, and some still do.

I started my first year there just as my brother was leaving. I say leaving, he didn't leave exactly; he was expelled. A teacher who we all called Piggy Bulloch asked him to take off his parka in class. My brother, being the belligerent teenager, quite rightly refused, because the school heating had broken down that day and it was minus ten and snowing outside. Even in those conditions, the principal wouldn't let the kids go home early, except for the ones who lived outside of town.

Apparently, Piggy had been standing over my brother and screaming at him for a full ten minutes to take off his coat, but Karl just stared out of the window, ignoring the nutter.

Something in Mr Piggy Bulloch snapped and he grabbed Karl by the scruff of his neck, dragging him up to his desk, and then screaming at him like a psychopath for a further fifteen minutes, demanding Karl hold out his hands for six of the best, which Karl was point-blank refusing to do.

The belt, normally known as the 'tweeg' at our school, was a heavy leather strap about a foot-and-a-half long and split into two at one end; a weapon designed especially to inflict as much pain as possible on disruptive teenagers without permanent disfigurement. Piggy Bulloch was notorious for dealing out the most painful of tweegings, although he often had to stand on his little piggy toes due to being a wee tubby pudding of a man.

Rather stupidly, my brother finally stuck out his hands and apparently took six of the best without flinching, but on the last strike gripped the leather belt in his burning fingers and yanked it from Piggy's grasp. He chucked it across the classroom, screaming, "FUCK YOU, YA PIGGY-FACED TWAT!" Then he smacked that fat fucker of a teacher so hard that he nearly put his little piggy nose on the other side of his piggy face. Blood spurted all over the kids sitting at the front of the class and Piggy collapsed in a shuddering heap.

That was it; my brother's school days had come to a predictably dismal end. Luckily for Karl, Piggy Bulloch dropped the charges, but his nose never looked the same again. Nor was he ever the same in himself after that little incident, retiring from teaching shortly afterwards. The rumour went around that he'd had a nervous breakdown of some sort and hit the bottle, and things had gone downhill rapidly from there. Although I hate to admit it, I always respected my brother for doing that, as we all did. Some of the teachers back then were total tyrants who should never have been allowed anywhere near teenagers or children. Bunch of cunts back in those days; what else can I say?

Our high school's claim to fame is that Monica Lewinsky spent a few years there, but in actual fact she only went to junior school in Thurso, while her parents were working at the nearby American naval base that was strategically placed to keep an eye on the Russians. However, there were some real freaks that did attend our school.

For example, there was Wee Stinky Jon, the son of a crofter who lived out in the sticks, in deepest, darkest, Caithness. Wee Jon absolutely stank and was a filthy little rascal. I'll never forget his podgy little hands, black with dirt and engine oil, which made his fingers look like little nicotine-stained claws. Put it this way, you would smell him before you'd see him, such was the rancid pong that came off the vile wee bugger. He could often be spotted in the school playground causing some sort of disruption or other, his usual smelly, half-smoked fag tucked behind his ear, dressed like some sort of medieval scarecrow, wearing massive rubber wellies with his dungarees pulled over them.

I always remember the time that he had a crowd of about twenty or so kids standing around him, all watching on in an amazed silence. He was standing completely still, like he was sneaking up on something, and then, all of a sudden he pounced like a ninja. Staring at him for a moment, I wondered what the hell was going on, only to realise with amazement that he had somehow managed to catch a living sparrow with his bare hands. Yes, Wee Stinky Jon was a master bird catcher! Kids would spend hours considering the odds and then betting their lunch money on whether or not Stinky Jon was able to catch a live bird that day. He usually could too, astonishingly enough.

Then there's another freak who comes to mind. We referred to him as Singing Simon. He was as mad as a box of frogs and he stank of fags too, but this was mostly overpowered by the sour pong of piss. Simon had tightly curled blond hair and looked exactly like a young, baby-faced 'Harpo' from the Marx Brothers. Simon came from one of the housing schemes across the river, where he lived with his mum. No one had ever heard him speak, and I mean *no one*, but boy, he could sing like an angel. Yep, he was a strange one alright.

One time when the teacher was out of the classroom, which happened a lot at our school, some of the class tormenters made Simon stand on a desk, ordering him to sing in front of the other kids or else take a good kicking. Of course, they did this knowing full well he had pissed himself again but it was easy to see that he was in no shape to take another kicking that day. So Simon stood up on the desk. I watched from the back of the class, and I couldn't help feeling sorry for the poor lad as the tears rolled down his sad wee pale face while all the kids screamed out: "SING, SING, SING, YA SMELLY TINK! SING, SING, SING, YA SMELLY TINK!"

Simon burst into song, and sang *Bright Eyes* from the film *Watership Down*, while a big wet piss-stain spread out on his purple velvet bell-bottom jeans and was clearly visible to the screeching girls who always sat at the front of the class. Despite his obviously distressed state, Simon's amazing singing reverberated around the cold concrete walls of the classroom, which gave it a haunting quality that quickly subdued the deafening rabble of hyperactive kids, until they sat listening in a spooky silence. As the words flowed out and around the room, the angelic sound of his voice brought most of the girls and dare I say a few of the boys to tears. It was so sad.

I don't mind admitting that his singing even brought a little tear to my own eye, as I watched his pitiful silhouette being lit up by a ray of sun that shone through the window, bathing him in pure white light. For a moment he looked like an unnamed saint, and we were all spellbound by the vision. Then the R.E. teacher walked in and pulled him down from the desk, slapped him in the back of the head and then locked him in the book cupboard for climbing on the furniture. Poor Simon.

Another eccentric who stands out in my memory was known around school as Pork Pie. You won't be surprised to learn that he got this name because of all the pork pies he could be seen shovelling into his fat gob at lunch breaks. Boy, he loved those pork pies; he was a proper addict!

Sometimes, if the notion took him, he would come into school wearing a long silk dress along with a big pair of steel toe-capped boots and a scruffy old Victorian top hat on his head! He was very weird and totally fearless. Wearing dresses and performing magic tricks made him a kind of endearing joker with all the girls, attention he obviously craved. The tough lads in the class hated him for this and would persistently tease him and interrupt his mind-boggling magic performances. Naturally, this would set him off into one of his frenzied rages wherein his face would turn a deep shade of purple, making his head look like it was about to explode. Even his tormenters were on their guard, knowing full well it was always a risky business disturbing one of Pork Pie's magic shows.

He was random as fuck, acting perfectly normally one moment and then doing something outrageous the next, like jumping out of a second floor window and nearly breaking his legs and back on the concrete playground below. He seemed to do these crazy things just for the hell of it, although I reckon they were always really done to get a giggle out of the girls. Pork Pie loved the girls, almost as much as pork pies. He had no issue with fighting either, since he was basically as hard as fuck. Personally, I thought he was alright, just a wee bit crazy.

Me and my mate Isaac were drinking cheap cider while sitting on some rocks near the beach one day, feeling bored shitless until we spotted Pork Pie rushing by. He was naked except for a very tight-fitting pair of Speedo swimming trunks that were yanked up to his flabby belly, and his skin was covered in what looked like thick lumps of lard or butter. We called him over, trying to hide our hysterics, but he was having none of it, shouting back in a determined voice, "Oot-ma-way-boys, I'm swimming to the Orkneys today!" Then he started singing, "I'm late! I'm late! For a very important date! No time to say hello, goodbye! I'm late! I'm late! I'm late!"

Our jaws hit the ground as we watched him belly-flop into the dark, freezing waves. Off he went, swimming in the direction of the Orkney Islands, which could be glimpsed through the mist on the far distant horizon. We grinned at each other, shook our heads and carried on drinking, taking the whole thing with a great big pinch of salt, which was a typical response when observing Pork Pie's off-the-wall antics. Anyway, we both agreed he was a pretty good swimmer considering he was such a fat fucker and the North Sea seemed fairly calm on that particular day. We left him to it and wandered off fairly soon after that.

Later on that week, while I was at my mum's house watching the local news on the TV with my feet up on the big

Freaks and Loners

leather pouffe, I nearly spilt my hot cup of tea all over myself in sheer disbelief as the newsreader started to describe how the body of a young man had been found washed up on the rocks near Holburn Head Lighthouse, a few miles away from Thurso beach. I stared at the picture they were showing on the television; it was Pork Pie! I couldn't believe it. What a very sad and peculiar way to go. I guess it was in true Pork Pie style though; oddball to the end.

Isaac and I were probably the last people to see him that day, before his demise. I've always felt a deep sense of guilt for not trying to stop him, but then again, how were we to know that the crazy fecker was going to go and get himself drowned? We'd just assumed it was another attention-seeking stunt and he'd be telling tales about it back at school soon enough. Of course, we kept our mouths shut.

Run, My little One, Run!

It will seem like every creature on this cursed earth will be your nemesis, for you are the innocence - the pure white light made flesh and fur. The target of a zillion EviL adversaries, and when they ensnare you with their nets and their traps, when their hounds tear at your flesh, they will take you half-ripped to shreds and cut off your paws and peel back your skin and feed their hellhounds your tiny beating heart as the life force slowly dissolves back into the great moor ready for resurrection; back to the shelter of the warren; the spiritual body of our Lord.

Let it be known that when our Lord raises a whisker there will be a glow in the sky, only then will the spit spray a million curses on our archenemies . . . the humans!

In the kingdom of our Lord the black bird sings as the eternal wheel of everlasting sorrow turns once again, as it always has, and always will. But first they must catch you. Run my little one, run!

The Power of Pussycats

Becoming aware of a recognisable scratching sound I strained to open my eyes, trying to make them focus in the darkened room; I jolted upright in the bed. Instantly spotting one of the farm cats meowing at my bedroom window; something this particular cat would often do. I pulled back the curtains momentarily blinding myself with a sudden burst of daylight as I reached out and let it in, seeing as it was still snowing and freezing out there. I love cats, but more than that, I love the feel of soft fur, and this was one of those big fluffy tabby cats that I had become good friends with since moving into the cottage.

This pussy was a vision of pure unadulterated perfection, but in a way that put me in a swoon, she/he was simply divine and perfect in every single furry way. I stood there in the darkened room wondering if I was still caught up in some sort of appalling dream within a dream within a dream within a dream . . . It was all too much for my fatigued brain - *I just need some furry love, that will sort me out*, I thought to myself while stroking the big furry moggy. I started rubbing my face into the soft fur as it rubbed up to me returning the love and affection, purring with more and more zeal. *Man, this old farm cat loves me and I love him/her*, I thought as I closed my eyes becoming immersed in the softness of its lovely, lovely fur.

Feeling yet another mind-expanding surge of Psilocin squeezing my brain, I opened my eyes again and quickly looked at my hand, fearing I was morphing into something. Thankfully, I was reassured when my hand appeared to look human-like. Then the notion of morphing into a cat really took hold of me, to the point where I surrendered and accepted that, *FUCK-IT, YES, I am now - a cat! Nothing wrong with that*, I thought, *being a cat is a very cool creature to be, actually*.

There were loads of reasons as far as I was concerned why being a cat was infinitely better than being Danny Texas - cancer survivor and professional procrastinator. *For example, cats live rent free, get free food, sleep as long as they want to, look great with no effort at all, have toes that look like cute oversized beans and have a license to kill anything smaller that moves. Also cats get to have loads and loads of sex - free love seemed to be the accepted path of the feline race, which has to be a good thing - right?*

At this point I couldn't contain myself any longer and held my paws up to the sky and screamed out loud, "I AM A CAT! I'M A BIG GORGEOUS SEXY CAT AND I'M PROUD OF IT! DO YOU HEAR ME? YOU BUNCH OF CUNTS! DO YOU HEAR ME? I - AM - PROUD!"

The bedroom door burst open and Tony came crashing in. I quickly looked over, it was clear by the crazed look on his face that he was tripping out of his mind, but I didn't care, I picked the cat up and went back to rubbing my face into his/her lovely soft fur once again. "Mmmm cats, I love cats, kitty, kitty-cat, pussy, meow, purr, purr, purr," I muttered to myself, lost in a moment of pure unadulterated love. Tony let out a shriek and called the rest of the boys to come and take a look. "This nutter is trying to make love to a cat, by-Christ!"

I scowled back at him, wondering what his fucking problem was, and then carried on rubbing my face into the soft, soft fur. To my shame I was so away with it believing I was cat-man I didn't notice that I was actually rubbing my face into the farm cat's fluffy arse. No wonder he/she was purring at me like that.

Snapping out of my delirium I began to realise that my face stank of smelly cat's arse. Immediately I ran to the bathroom sink and stuck my face under the tap, scrubbing at it while yacking up furry fluff balls that had got stuck in the back of my throat. *How the fuck does my mouth taste like this - what the hell have I been doing?* I thought to myself, horrified.

After yacking up more fluff balls I took a quick look at myself in the bathroom mirror, I was somewhat disappointed to see that my suspicions were right - I did indeed appear to have someone else's teeth in my mouth, but they weren't human teeth, no, they were more like . . . rabbit teeth!? I wasn't a cat at all - I was a fucking rabbit!

Letting out a pathetic whimper, I stepped back from the mirror in absolute horror as my pals fell about on the floor laughing like a bunch of evil little fleecy-looking motherfuckers with big ears who were secretly conspiring a campaign of mental torture within me for the sheer play of it. *The sneaky cunts!* I took another quick look in the mirror. I was Danny again except for the teeth. *This is some heavy shit*, I thought.

My mood changed and I started laughing, quickly realising that these were my pals and that there was nothing to really worry about, even if I was acting mental. I stopped laughing. Stepping out of the bathroom, taking a quick look around the room, then walking over to the bedroom door mumbling some excuses about needing to sort my head out. No one seemed at all interested; too preoccupied with laughing. I didn't care what was going on in my living room anymore, they were all welcome to it as far I was concerned. I shut the door and fell onto the bed like a sack of spuds, closed my eyes, and drifted into another strange psychedelic daze of random accounts of my fractured past.

Isaac's Birthday Present

High school could have been a nice experience, but it wasn't. To me it felt like there was something evil emanating from the very land that it was built upon. Brutality, usually coming in the form of physical and emotional torture, was dished out on a daily basis like it was some special rite of passage for unassuming wimps, weird loners and the damaged ones who wandered the school playground on lunch breaks. This was how the school tormenters passed their days; prowling around like a pack of psychotic mongrels orchestrating a mini crime wave, continually intimidating one poor fucker or another at any given opportunity.

I was fairly lucky, in that if anyone hassled me I would get protection from the Dooley boys. They were my pals, especially Isaac who was hard as nails, but I didn't see him like that generally. He was just my pal and we got on, even though he was a few years older than me.

One time we were trying out a new air rifle that he had been given for his sixteenth birthday, by shooting at a few wild rabbits. It didn't take long for Isaac to hit one. As we walked toward to the dying bunny, Isaac swiftly reloaded the rifle on the off-chance that the creature would make a run for it. When we got there we could see that the rabbit had taken a pellet directly to the back of its tiny skull. The poor thing was writhing in pain from its head injury and letting out a horrible yelping sound. Isaac told me to hold the gun but to be careful as it was loaded.

I watched on as he skilfully tugged on the rabbit's hind legs with one hand and pulled on its ears with his other. There was a clicking sound as its tiny neck broke. It seemed that was it, but then the rabbit let out a shocking high-pitched squeal as the life seeped out of its little body. Flinching at the sound, I accidentally squeezed the trigger of the gun, which happened to be pointing directly at Isaac's jaw as he crouched over the dead rabbit. The crack of the shot stunned me. Isaac flew backwards, arms flailing toward his face, and collapsed.

"FUCK!" I screamed.

Time froze, but my mind raced at a zillion miles an hour. *Fucking hell, I've just shot Isaac Dooley in the face at close range with his own gun! On his birthday!* Isaac lay on the ground, his hands over his face, motionless. The awful reality of the situation drained all the blood from my arms and legs. *Oh my God, I've fucking killed him!*

The realisation felt like a shard of ice being driven into my chest. I started to shake violently, letting the air rifle fall to the ground. Then a groaning sound came from behind Isaac's now blood-soaked hands. *Even if I haven't killed him,* I thought, *he is Isaac Dooley; he will surely kick the living shite out of me! And then his brothers will kill me for sure.* My brain grappled with the horror of it all. I took a half-step towards him, my hands outstretched. "Isaac, I'm sorry, it was a pure accident, are you okay?" Isaac still didn't move and I could see blood running freely over his knuckles. Then he started to rock to and fro in pain. "You've blin me, min!" came his muffled, pained reply.

"I'm sorry, it was a pure accident. Are you okay?" It was all I could think to ask. I was horrified.

"Fucking quit asking if I'm okay! Do I look okay? Ya daft wee cunt, ye!" As he spoke, he slowly pulled his blood-soaked hands away from his face, while scanning with his tongue like crazy to see what the damage was. He wiped the blood from his eyes with his sleeve and blinked, trying to focus on me. Then the bugger stuck out his clenched, bloodied fist towards me. I flinched slightly, but to my amazement he slowly opened his hand and there in his palm sat a squashed, metal pellet.

As I looked more closely at the mess of his face, I could see the pellet had gone through his bottom lip and, as I found out in more detail later, had come to rest in the roof of his mouth. He'd managed to work the thing out while rocking about on the grass. To add to my absolute bewilderment, he started grinning at me while the blood still oozed down his face and neck. "I cannae believe it, Danny, you shot me in the fucking gob, ya numpty!" he said with some difficulty, his torn lip flapping and his tongue rapidly swelling up.

"I'm really sorry, Isaac, honest to Christ I didnae mean it," I pleaded, thinking I was going to get a proper hiding. He shook his head at me, chuckled in astonishment, and then got to his knees. He picked up the dead rabbit with one hand and we put it in a plastic shopping bag. I helped him to his feet. He flipped the air rifle at me with the toe of his boot, and so I nervously picked it up again, making sure not to put my fingers anywhere near the trigger. Then we slowly walked back to his house, both stunned by what had just taken place.

Thankfully, in the end Isaac only had to have some stitches in his lip, though it swelled up like a golf ball, making him look like a ginger freak. Surprisingly, Isaac was a good sport about the matter and for whatever reason thought the whole thing was hilarious, continually thanking me because it got him out of school for a full month.

About three weeks after this crazy drama, I was walking to *Cardosis*, our local sweet shop, along with Isaac and his cousin, Andy Bean. Andy kept banging on about how jealous he was of Isaac getting all that time off school and how he wished he could get off school too. Then he came up with the hare-brained idea of getting Isaac to punch him in the eye, so he could say to his teacher that he'd had an accident and couldn't see properly. Isaac looked at him for a moment then said bluntly, "Nah, I'm not doing it." Andy kept going on and on and on about it until - SMACK! - Isaac, without any warning, punched Andy so hard he knocked him out, breaking his jaw and cheekbone in two places. Andy got a whole three months off of school and, once he could talk again, thanked his cousin for sorting him out! Heh - crazy fuckers.

Aye, they were proper fierce, them Dooley boys. Sometimes, Thurso would remind me of one of those cowboy ghost towns out in the arse-end of the Wild West, with the Dooley boys being like the cowboys I had seen in those old black and white movies our dad would make us watch on rainy Sunday afternoons. You know those scenes where you would see them eating baked beans from a tin plate with a wooden spoon as they all sat around a campfire, with the moody sound of a harmonica being played softly in the background.

Well, the only difference is that the Dooley boys would all be sprawled on a knackered old sofa in their back garden, eating beans from paper plates with plastic spoons, while watching a car tyre burn in a rusty old oil drum, to the soundtrack of their parents screaming at each other from within the depths of their shabby house.

One of the funniest memories I have of being a teenager in Thurso was when I was out one day with a few of the Dooley boys, mucking about and smashing stuff up in an old deserted farmhouse down by Thurso river, having some fun with an old lump hammer that we had found by the side of the railway line. We were just doing what young working-class lads from the scheme did when trying to break up the monotony of a long, boring summer's day; a bit of pointless vandalism.

Then, random as you like, Isaac came up with the brainwave of luring a gang of kids from the scheme down to this old house to play Ouija board, which was a bit of a teenage craze back in those days. The plan was that Isaac would conduct the séance, while Andy, Davie (Isaac's older brother) and I would hide in the house, secretly waiting for the other kids to partake in their Ouija board session, with the aim of terrifying the fuck out of them all. Ouija boards, demons and ghosts were all the rage when we were kids, thanks to films like *The Exorcist* and *The Omen*, which we had all seen.

Anyway, most of the kids knew about this old house, since it was rumoured that a murder had been committed there many years ago, which is why it was supposed to be properly haunted. So, off Isaac went, disappearing for ages while rounding up a load of kids and daring them to come down to the old house by the river to try to call up the Devil via a homemade Ouija board, just for the craic.

As dusk was setting in we spotted him heading back down through the fields with about twenty kids, all revved up for scaring the shit out of themselves. Of course, this was a chance for the boys to show how tough and brave they were in front of the girls. We stayed hidden and silent as they all arrived at the house and carefully picked their way up the remnants of the rotten, broken staircase to the first floor.

Once they had all settled down, a few candles were placed around the room, making shadows flicker over the shabby, half-stripped walls and the damp old bits of wallpaper hanging from them. It was a suitably creepy atmosphere. With everyone gathered around an improvised table, on top of which sat a roughly fashioned Ouija board, Isaac started calling out to the spirits. Fingers were placed on a jam jar and the nervously excited kids waited for a response. The candles flickered some more as a gentle breeze blew through the broken windows, making a low whistling sound. The girls giggled nervously, only to be shushed by Isaac who was pretending to be focused on making the spirits move the glass.

Of course, Isaac deliberately moved the glass to spell out the word *Satan*. The girls all seemed to buy into the deception and started giggling nervously again. The boys, on the other hand, raised eyebrows at each other, suspecting that Isaac was having them all on. Isaac called out to the spirits once more, a sly smile on his face, knowing full well that Andy, Davie and I were all hiding in the cavities between the rotting plaster walls at the far end of the large room. He called out again, giving us the cue. "Are there any spirits present? We come in peace and mean you no harm. Please, if you are there, make yourselves known. Move the jar or knock on the table!"

There was a pause as everyone held their breath, nervousness etched on the girls' faces in the flickering light. Andy gently tapped twice on the wall he was hiding behind, and everybody froze. He tapped again, but this time a little harder. There were a few suppressed squeals as all the kids started looking around the room, peering into the gloom, trying to find the source of the noise. Then Davie let out an eerie whisper and I joined in by punching my hand straight through the thin plaster wall.

The kids completely freaked out. The boys took flight, some so terrified that they jumped out of the first floor windows. Girls ran round in the darkness, screaming hysterically, banging into walls and doors, looking for ways out of the house. Some of them went into a terrified huddle, holding onto each other and screaming the place down. So just for a bit of added fun, I punched my other hand through the plaster wall, making one of them go into a full-on panic attack, which resulted in her peeing herself.

Naturally, we fell about in total hysterics, while at the same time trying to calm down the screaming girls who were now frantic. I ran to the window and watched the rest of the screaming kids legging it through the moonlit fields like startled bunny rabbits. I'd never seen anything like it. Hilarious! Still, good old instant karma bit us on the arse for playing that little practical joke; just as we had finally managed to calm the remaining girls down a bit, Isaac fell through some rotting floorboards and broke his ankle, which meant we had to carry the fucker all the way home through the fields in the darkness, which took hours.

Three Emissaries!

With three twitches of a whisker, three emissaries we shall send!

To one with red hair, a black heart and a rusted blade we shall lend our keenest ear; let him hear their very thoughts! Let him spoil all cheer with spit, spite and fear! Let him lead them to misfortune!

For a second we shall raise up a tormented soul from the darkness of the Great Black Warren. Let the cursed spirit carry the slaughtered souls of the innocents as his burden! Let him cross their crooked path and let the stench of sour tobacco make them heave and retch!

Then a third we shall conceal inside the severed skull of a martyred one. A winged demon shall rise from the rotting flesh, spitting curses and laying its foul seed in the jellied brains of the martyred ones! Let its black maggots feed on the flesh of those who persecute and murder us! Let its dreadful buzzing drive the murderers to ruin, madness and death!

Avenge the martyred ones!
Avenge the martyred ones!
Avenge the martyred ones!

Giant Brown Slug!

Ding-dong. Ding-dong. Ding-dong. I woke for a moment, and then closed my eyes again, thinking it was a dream. Ding-dong. Ding-dong. DING-DONG! I woke again, shook my head, and then slipped back into sleep. Ding-dong. Ding-dong. DING-FUCKING-DONG! I came to, more fully. DING-DONG! DING-DONG! DING-FUCKING-DONG! Irritation swept me up into full consciousness. "Fucking ding-dong, ding-dong, DING-FUCKING-DONG! WHO THE FUCK IS PLAYING WITH THE DOORBELL!? FOR THE LOVE OF CHRIST, I'M TRYING TO SLEEP, YA BUNCH OF BASTARDS!" I was pure exasperated.

I leapt up from the bed and wrenched opened the bedroom door, glancing wildly around the living room. My mood changed immediately as I saw how Tony, Fergus, Wallace and Cormag were all huddled on the sofa, looking totally terrified as they watched Jerry swing his arms, except this time there were no arms; all I could see were multi-coloured tracers moving at a super-sonic speed, like the blurred wings of a huge insect. It was so strange and mesmerizing to watch, and I stood motionless, lost in the moment, my rage suspended as I witnessed this voodoo shit playing out before my marble-sized eyes. Reality was on hold once again.

Ding-dong. Ding-dong. Ding-dong. Ding-dong. The doorbell began ringing like crazy again, snapping me out of it. *Stop pressing the doorbell, you cunt! I don't give a shit if it is my front door; I'm not answering it, now fuck-off!* I screamed inwardly. At least, I thought it was inwardly. Jerry stopped swinging his arms, looked straight at me with genuine concern on his face, and then asked me if I wanted him to go and see who it was. I nodded back at him, without speaking, while trying to contain my frustration at the situation. Ding-dong. Ding-dong. The doorbell rang again. Jerry made his way to the front door as if he were perfectly sober.

The others were now staring at me, looking like they were all about to take off, or burst into tears, or possibly both. "What's up wi' you lot?" I snapped at them, and they all flinched at the same time, open mouths closing. Fergus responded, "Did ye not see the speed that radge's arms were moving? Did ye not see it?"

"Aye, I seen it . . . Pretty cully, right enough," I muttered back, wondering to myself how anyone could possibly swing their arms that fast. Tony interrupted the general train of thought, "Danny I don't mean to be disrespectful or anything, mate, but has anybody ever told you, um, well, that you look a wee bit like a gnome? You're nothing like a cat at all."

The others started giggling like little childish brats and for a moment I felt a bit hurt by this comment. "You're tripping out, ya eejits. You took magic mushrooms, remember?" Cormag suddenly pulled an odd facial expression, then he went into more fits of laughter, acting like he had seen something whoosh by; his eyes were lit up like candles. Wallace looked at him, puzzled like the rest of us, and then quietly asked, "Are ye alright?"

Cormag replied, calm but confused, "Can you see it?"

"See what?" asked Fergus.

Cormag looked at us all for a moment as if we were all daft. "The flow of energy flushing through the house! It looks like white noise except it's pink, red and grey. . . Can ye not see it?" We all shook our heads; it was clear that none of us had a clue what the hell he was banging on about. Then, the mumbling going on at the front door drew my attention away.

Immediately, I started to worry that maybe it was those *Banana Splits* radges with their daft moon buggies, trying to sweet-talk their way into my tiny house. *Please, God, don't let it be them, they'll wreck the place; they're manic as fuck!* My mind raced with fresh dread at the very thought of it all. I looked over at Fergus; he looked back at me and gave me a really worrying nod of the head.

Then, the door banged shut, and as random as you like, 'Chong' the drug-dealer stepped into my living room, looking as shifty as fuck. Nothing unusual about that of course, but it put a whole new spin on the dynamics of the situation, not to mention creating an instantly unpleasant atmosphere. Something about this guy always got my hackles up. *What the fuck does he want?* The question rattled around my skull as I tried to act normal in front of the creepy twat.

He reached out his hand and I went for a handshake, only to realise that he was actually trying to give me a knuckle-touch. But it was too late and I panicked and grabbed his fist, and then rather stupidly, I shook it. Chong looked ill at ease for moment, staring at my hand wrapped around his scabby, freezing fist. He smirked at me as if I was totally bonkers. Tony, Fergus, Wallace and Cormag all gave Chong knuckles, acting like a bunch of cool kiddies and as if they were sober all of a sudden. Jerry did the same, and then carried on swinging his arms at an uncanny velocity. Chong seemed unfazed by Jerry's peculiar behaviour, while the others were all briefly sucked in again, mesmerised.

Slightly miffed at my inability to be hip, I stood there while my internal monologue ranted on about how much I hated all that American cool-kiddie high-five bollocks. *What's wrong with a good old traditional handshake, eh?* I asked myself rhetorically, immediately wincing at how un-hip that sounded in my own head. I tried to act like I was unruffled, raising an eyebrow at my gang of daft pals as they vainly tried to pretend to Chong that they were easily handling the black brew.

Then my attention fixed on our unwelcome guest, who looked like a character straight out of a Dickens story, all hunched up in his shabby old Afghan coat, with a grubby rainbow-coloured scarf wrapped around his long scrawny neck, and an ill-fitting hunting cap pulled tightly over a mass of thick, ginger dreadlocks. His head was seriously looking more and more like a witch doctor's rattle every time I saw him; clearly an effect of the long-term use of hard drugs.

He always stank of patchouli oil fused with the intense pong of body odour, and you could tell he didn't changed his clothes much, let alone wash them or himself, for that matter. In spite of this already colourful stench, there was an additional musty, egg-like pong that came from his ginger dreadlocks. They were stuck together in thick, dandruff-encrusted clumps that hung down his back. To finish the look, he sported a pair of massive orange side-burns that were way too dominant for his sickly, pale face.

No, Chong wasn't pretty, and wasn't exactly a friend either; he was just some dodgy fuck from whom I occasionally bought hash. He was from Edinburgh originally, and supposedly had some big-time connections there. We all knew he was a serious junkie with unpredictable, psychopathic tendencies, who suffered from a delusion that he had powers of telepathy. He did have the ability to creep you out with his beady-eyed stare, as if he was trying to read your thoughts, but we all knew this was total bollocks really, just another strand of self-aggrandising bullshit put about by a scumbag permanently high on a cocktail of dirty drugs. None of us really trusted the toe rag, giving him the body-swerve whenever possible.

In spite of this, he did have his uses when it came to scoring a bit of quality hashish. In truth, we were all shit-scared of him. Chong was pretty intimidating and unpredictable and we all secretly hated the wanker, although we pretended otherwise to his face. So I was never that thrilled to see him, but for some reason, I took his arrival in the middle of our massive trip as a particularly bad omen. I couldn't shake the feeling that there was something extra sinister about him today, like he'd been blown here on some ill wind and for no good purpose. Wherever Chong went, you could guarantee something bad would happen; trouble just seemed to follow him around. I guess he was just bad to the bone.

He didn't have a single redeeming trait that I could think of, and I can honestly say that I had never heard him utter a kind word about anyone or anything. *Oh well, at least it wasn't those Banana Splits wankers,* I thought, trying to convince myself that things would be alright, secretly hoping that Chong was only paying us a flying visit, even though I knew Chong didn't really do flying visits and always outstayed his 'welcome'. Still, we all put on a façade and pretended to be his mate. It was just easier that way. This was one psychopath you didn't want get on the wrong side of.

Feeling pretty hesitant, I parked my arse on a chair while keeping a watchful eye on him as he made himself comfortable on the floor, next to my precious vinyl collection. He started flicking through the records, chuckling to himself in a typically creepy way. Tactfully, I asked him to put something mellow on, seeing as we were all tripping out. The others stared at Chong in complete silence as he smiled over at me in his familiar, unsettling manner, and then he proceeded to pick out a record.

Now, it's a well-known fact among those who know me that one of my pet hates is anyone messing with my vinyl without due care. Having to witness that smelly freak manhandling my records while I was in such a precarious state of mind was bringing me close to a panic attack as my OCD started getting the better of me. My eyes never left the twat for a second.

Thankfully, he picked *Adventures Beyond The Ultraworld* by The Orb. *Perfect choice*, I thought. Watching on in silence, I felt a twitch behind my eyes as he yanked the record out of its inner sleeve and plonked it onto the moving record deck. The dopey fucker then dropped the stylus out of his pathetically quivering grip and onto the vinyl, making a loud thump that popped through the speakers. The others ducked and jumped, wondering what was going on. *Total fanny!* my inner voice screamed, as I clocked him making himself comfortable once again by leaning against my stack of precious records and using the empty album cover to skin up on. *You disrespectful wanker, that's my Adventures Beyond The Ultraworld getting ruined there,* I muttered inside myself, trying hard not to react to the twat, seeing as I was tripping out like a lab-chimp with a battery-operated butt-plug up my arse.

Chong was well known for taking offence easily, which mostly led to crazy outbursts of psychotic, paranoid ranting that often ended in senseless acts of horrific violence. It was a matter of fact that Chong was a psycho and more than capable of murder. We all knew what he was like when he started kicking off, which can be summed up in two words; scary fucker.

Out of the corner of my eye, I noticed him spilling tobacco and bits of discarded roach all over my floor, showing absolutely no regard for the fact that this was *my* house. He had appalling manners and at that moment in time I dearly wished that I had the guts to grab him by the scruff and boot him out the door.

On the other hand, I knew if I attempted such an act he would go bonkers and probably stab me up and stamp on my head, like we'd all witnessed him doing once to some drunken guy who'd jumped the queue at the bar in our local pub. Luckily for Chong, the police had been kept out of it and the crime had been quickly covered up. Everyone who'd witnessed it had turned a blind eye, including the drunken guy who'd been stabbed in the arm, although this was probably also due in part to him having his head stamped several times as he fell to the ground, knocking him unconscious for about ten minutes. Chong had acted like he was trying to pop a balloon at a kid's party.

Jerry spotted what was going on, he stopped swinging his arms and sat himself down. Fishing out his rusty old smoking tin he filled up my bong with large amounts of squidgy-black hash and passed it over, giving me a wink. Holding the plastic bong in my quivering hand, I put my mouth up to it and took a long hard pull and then released a rather impressive plume of smoke into the air. It was times like this that made me realise how lucky I was to have a pal like Jerry. Naturally, we all did a few large bongs each. The calming effect of the marijuana hit us like a sack of fluffy feathers and everything was chilled.

The room didn't feel so sinister anymore, in fact, nothing did. We all nodded our heads in time to *Little Fluffy Clouds*, the perfect soundtrack. It didn't bother me that all my pals now looked like they'd morphed into long-eared fluff balls with whiskers and annoying twitchy noses; I was okay with it. I actually started to feel mild waves of euphoria pulsing through my body even though I was still hallucinating like a motherfucker. The trick was to try not to focus on any one thing for too long, because as soon as I did, things started morphing into all sorts of weird stuff; everything seemed to be alive.

Fearing that Chong might catch on to my distaste for him, I thought it best to make some light conversation with the tosser, and without being too direct, I tried to find out what had prompted this delightful visit. His story was that he was belatedly delivering some hash that I had apparently pre-ordered many weeks ago, although I had no memory of ever having such a conversation with the fanny.

This of course, was perfectly normal behaviour for a paranoid drug dealer who was constantly spaced out of his box on amphetamines, heroin and God knows what else, and in my current state I really wasn't in a position to trust my own memory very much either. Sitting across from him I could see he was in poor shape; the dark rings under his eyes told a sorry story of days, possibly weeks, of sleep deprivation. Chong was always scrawny looking, even before he got into hard drugs, but he was now starting to look horribly anorexic. Although we'd been acquainted for eight years or so, I couldn't recall ever seeing him eating food.

True to form, he started cutting up large lines of amphetamine on my coffee table, scratching the table's surface to bits with a nasty looking knife that seemed to have a real rabbit's foot for a handle. I tried to ignore the furry foot that seemed to me to be twitching and straining with a life of its own, working Chong's hand around the table, and instead looked around at my pals who seemed somewhat taken aback at the sight of the massive lump of amphetamine crystal he had casually produced from his coat pocket. Once he'd snorted up his share, he offered it to us all.

We all looked at each other and I believe in that moment we all thought as one mind: *fuck-it, sing hosannas and break out the dry sherry!* None of us were very good at saying no to free drugs, especially when Chong was the one offering; that would be like saying no to Charlie Manson, that famous icon of evil with whom I felt Chong inadvertently had a lot in common.

Yes, there was something about him showing up like this and crashing our wee party that was filling me with dread. There was always a nagging feeling of doom whenever he was around me, but today it seemed more pointed. *He always turns up like a bad penny,* I thought, finding myself dwelling once more on the idea of his so-called telepathic abilities. Secretly, I watched his unblinking eyes taking in everyone's body language, scanning for weaknesses to home in on. He was after something, I was sure of it!

Inevitably we got caught up in a mammoth speed session with the dodgy fucker, as he cut up line after line, scratching my coffee table some more. *Alison is going to go nuts when she sees those scratches,* I found myself worrying, but common sense prevailed and I turned a blind eye to it, knowing full well that he would take offence if I moaned at him about it and that upsetting her was probably the lesser of two evils in this case.

When I got around to asking him for the hash that I had apparently ordered, he started checking all his pockets looking baffled, then went on to pulling apart his bag for a bit, until eventually he gave me a blank look, shrugged his shoulders and mumbled back at me without breaking eye contact that he must have left it at home.

Time started speeding up while Chong went on to tell us that he was in a bit of a situation, having spent the last day and a half tearing his house apart looking for three kilos of amphetamine that he had (apparently) stashed in one of his many hiding places, but being a spacey fecker, he couldn't remember exactly where. The scary part was that he had a bunch of Edinburgh gangsters offering to cut off his fingers if he didn't find the money for it within forty-eight hours. Daily reality was a chaotic mess for Chong; he was dealing large amounts of drugs around the town in order to feed his own greedy habit. It was clear to me, and to all who knew him, that his life was seriously messed up. On the sly, I continued to watch his every move, not trusting him for one moment.

He asked if he could grab a beer from the fridge, I told him to help himself and, daringly, asked him to grab me one while he was at it. He gave me a hollow look as he got up, then he casually started body-popping across the room in time to the music, breaking into fits of freaky dancing in the middle of my kitchen. We all watched on, moderately bemused by the nutty behaviour of the creep. Although I hate to admit it, he could really move, but still, the sight of him made me vow to myself that I would never go as far down this route of drugged-up debauchery as he obviously had.

This was a guy whose dignity had been steadily swept away by the drug-fuelled tornado that had whirled through the early 1990s. Chong was on the edge of complete self-destruction, an observation that was reinforced for me when he unwittingly pulled up his coat sleeves, exposing horribly bruised arms that were all scabby and infected from injecting drugs badly. Mesmerised, I looked on as he pranced around my kitchen, flying off his tits and looking, as I said before, like a witchdoctor's rattle wearing a waxed-cotton hunting cap. *Pathetic twat*, I thought.

Drugs, drugs, drugs; will it ever end? The thought induced feelings of guilt as I started sensing the next wave of hallucinations taking hold again, but the question seemed to answer itself straight away. *Nae bother, bring it on,* said an opposing voice, while tendrils of pure delight rippled throughout my body, again and again.

Then my tripped-out unease lifted once more and everything felt really upbeat, even if we did look like a bunch of demoralised also-rans from the most remote housing scheme in the coldest, most forsaken county of the dispossessed. Still, I couldn't help noticing how fleecy everyone's skin was looking, like there was some kind of weird furriness to everyone's appearance. *And what's all that nose twitching about?* I asked myself before concluding that; *maybe it's the amphetamines kicking in.* One thing was for sure; normality was still being very much kept at bay.

Gazing over at the clock on the kitchen wall I was shocked to see it was now nearly-five thirty and it was getting pretty dark outside. Then it hit me that we were supposed to be getting charged up for the gig of our lives, but as I gazed around the room and took in just how spacey everyone looked, I concluded that this particular mission had been accomplished.

Chong started quizzing me about the Pope gig; he had never heard any of Peggy's music, being heavily into acid-house and rave music at the time. Getting up from my chair

I reached over to my record collection and picked out Peggy Pope's seventh album. Carefully, I put away my *Adventures Beyond The Ultraworld* record, cunningly brushing off all the bits of tobacco and tiny specs of squidgy-black hash into the kitchen bin and then quickly checking for any damage done to the cover.

Annoyingly, Chong picked up the Peggy album cover, looked at it for a few moments, smiled while raising an eyebrow, and then started to use *it* to skin up on. I secretly gave the cunt daggers as I watched him spill more bits of tobacco and hash all over it. *Fucking philistine!* I screamed at the wanker from inside my head, but despite my pent-up frustration I have to confess that my heart was racing in a rather pleasing manner. I felt a sudden jolt of euphoria race up and down my spine, a nice feeling, I may add.

The speed had obviously kicked in because everyone was now chit-chatting away at each other like a bunch of grannies at the bingo. There was no doubt in my mind that I was still tripping my nuts off while taking a sip of beer that gently turned into a chomp, I still had misgivings about my teeth, they just didn't feel right anymore, but I was too scared to go to a mirror and check it out, knowing full well it would trip my head out even more than it already was.

Tony, Fergus, Wallace and Cormag were still squeezed together on the sofa grinning and yacking away at each other about random shit that none of them were actually really listening to. Then the room would go into quiet spells of silence as heads nodded in time to the music that swelled and bounced around the open plan living area of my house. I watched on as Chong reached into his scabby old bag and pulled out a brown bottle, took the lid off and spilled some large red and yellow pill capsules onto the table. "Ten quid a pop, boys, and worth every penny, by the way!" he announced with an evil grin on his skeletal face.

"What are they?" asked Fergus.

"Rhubarb and Custards!" replied Chong, with a stagnant smirk on his face.

"Ecstasy?" Tony asked in a bemused tone of voice.

"Sure is," replied Chong, looking rather smug.

Now, it is probably worth pointing out that none of us had ever tried Ecstasy, but we had all heard and read about this new wonder drug that was now driving a new wave of pleasure-seeking debauchery among British youth culture in the 1990s. Before I knew what was what, we were all digging out tenner notes from our pockets and wallets. The Rhubarb and Custard capsules were down my pals' throats without giving it a second thought, tensely I looked on, and then gulped my one down with a big glug of crispy beer.

Chong necked three of the capsules in a oner and for a moment we all got a little concerned, fearing the junkie fucker had gone one step too far. All of us watched on in silence, secretly fearing that he was going to pass out. His facial features started contorting and twitching in a very disturbing manner, then, thankfully, that vile clown-grin reached across his pale face as he let out a shudder of deep inner bliss. His eyes visibly lit up as euphoria rippled through his withered body, making him twitch some more. He stood up and did some more body popping, switching to the robot, then back to body popping, and then finishing off with a perfectly executed Michael Jackson moonwalk.

Without warning the first inklings of what can only be described as sheer bliss spread like wild fire, creating a real sensation of communion among us all. Yet inexplicably, there was also a sense of electricity flying around the room stirring up waves of purpose and empathy. I knew this was the counterfeit love I had read about with regards to this trendy new designer drug. We all shook our heads at each other not really knowing what to say, all of us feeling properly blissed-out of our boxes for the first time in our lives.

I gazed over at Chong as he did a perfect backspin on the kitchen floor that momentarily made him look like a massive spinning coin. *Maybe he's not so bad after all?* I thought. But I quickly put myself in check, knowing instinctively that he was nothing but trouble and at some point in the night we'd all have to lose the prick or he would just get us all caught up in his sketchy reality. There was no doubt in my mind that him showing up out of the blue like this was indeed a bad, bad omen.

All at once I became conscious of needing a pee, so I made a dash for the toilet, slamming the door behind me and then frantically twiddling the lock until it finally bolted. After some disarray trying to get the zip on my jeans to work I had the most pleasurable piss I have ever experienced in my whole life. One thing about tripping out on mushrooms is that they make you pee a lot, but this combined with ecstasy and speed was a whole other experience, which is rather difficult to describe.

I took a quick look in the mirror. My eyes were black marbles; this was to be expected, but it scared me slightly to see my teeth looking so abnormally big. *You're tripping out, Danny, it's not real*, I reminded myself as I gazed at my reflection for a bit, while my thoughts became slowly distracted by the hullabaloo of my pals on the other side of the bathroom door. "Right, I'd better try and get my shit together seeing as we are off to see Mr Pope tonight!" I mumbled to myself as a sudden sense of urgency entered into my head. Another pleasurable rush of excitement steamed through my body again, and for a few lost seconds I felt fantastic! "I know, I'll run a bath and scrub up seeing as we are having a wild night out. Stop talking to yourself, Danny, that's what crazy people do, and you are not crazy; just high on drugs!" This made me stop talking out aloud. *I'd better inform them that I'm getting ready for the gig,* I muttered to myself, but this time inside my head.

After some fussing with the toilet lock I stuck my head out of the bathroom door, yelling over the din to the others that I was going to freshen up before we headed out. They all gave me the thumbs up except for Jerry who looked really upset for a moment, and then came over. "Where are you going, Danny?" he yelled in my ear.

"To the gig," I yelled back in his.

"What gig?" he barked, looking really puzzled.

"The Pope gig, of course," I barked back.

"When are you coming back then?" he snapped.

"You're coming with me, aren't you?" I snapped back, getting really worried that the fucker wasn't going to come to the gig for some reason. Bamboozled for a moment, I watched Jerry's face slowly light up as the confusion drifted off like a mist.

"Oh, yeah, the Pope gig, I forgot about all that," he yelled back in my ear, then looked at me blankly trying to hide his bewilderment.

I looked at him and then asked in a softer voice, "What's up?"

His face went blank for a second and then he asked, "Have we got tickets for this Pope gig then?"

Nodding back while rolling my eyes at the spaced-out numpty, there was an awkward pause as I watched the penny gradually drop; I gave him a defiant look. Gently, I shut the door, walked over to the bathtub and turned the hot tap on to run a bath for myself, even though I knew the water would only be warmish at best. I took another really long enjoyable piss in the toilet, childishly aiming at the skid-marks on the inside of the toilet pan as my emotions meandered from apprehension to exhilaration; I was loaded like a motherfucker, and I knew it! The toilet pan started throbbing and pulsating, I looked away and shook my head for a moment, squirming to keep a hold of reality.

I decided to light a few scented candles after spying them on the shelf by the window then I switched off the main light. Almost immediately the flickering candlelight had a pleasant, calming effect on me, giving a real sense of warmth in the freezing cold bathroom. The heating was rubbish in our cottage, it only ever came on randomly, so everything relied on the wood burner to get any real warmth flowing around the house.

Once the bath was run I lowered myself in gently, relaxing in the warm water. *The first time I've felt proper warmth all day*, I thought to myself. The sensation of the water around my naked body worked well with the cocktail of chemicals that flushed through my veins. Everything felt tip-top and nothing mattered anymore, life seemed perfect for a few lost moments relaxing there with my eyes closed, feeling the love vibrating all over me like I was back in the womb again.

Then typically and without any warning whatsoever Tony burst through the door that I had stupidly forgotten to lock, looking really troubled, then, blasé as you like, the radge pulled his trousers down and proceeded to take a shit in the toilet right next me, "Oi, oi, what's your fucking game, eh?" I shouted at him.

GIANT BROWN SLUG!

Tony looked at me with a relieved look on his face as horrible squirting farts came from his arse. "Sorry, Danny, I forgot you were having a bath, hope you don't mind? I've got the shits really bad today for some reason." Then the cheeky bastard got off the toilet and shamelessly wiped his arse right in front of me. Looking on aghast and totally dumbstruck as my eyes caught sight of his scary silhouetted shadow against the wall behind him - not a pretty sight, I may add!

He pulled his trousers up and washed his hands in my bath, and then he casually asked me why I had an enormous slug stuck to my leg? I didn't pay much attention to his random question, as I was more preoccupied with the awful smell coming from the shit-splashed toilet right next to me. "You skanky bastard, get the fuck out! I'm trying to have a bath - Jesus Christ, man, have you got no moral fibre or pride in yourself, eh?" my spluttered response; a combination of nausea and total disbelief as the reek of shit hit the back of my throat. Tony just gave me an arrogant smile then the cheeky bugger dried his hands on my bath towel, shrugged his shoulders and sauntered backwards while grinning at me like a melon on peyote, and then he shut the bathroom door gently behind him.

Glancing down at my leg I couldn't quite grasp what I was seeing for a split second. To my absolute horror there was a huge brown slug that was at least the breadth of a well-fed sparrow and as long as a cucumber slithering its way up my inner thigh, towards my bare bollocks. "ARGGHHH! ARGGHHH! ARGGHHH!" I launched myself out of the bath, falling backwards through the bathroom door, landing flat on my arse with the giant slug still stuck to my inner thigh as the others yelled out, wondering what the hell was going on with me.

"ARGGHHH! ARGGHHH! ARGGHHH! Get it off me, please, get it, OFF! ARGGHHH, PLEASE, ARGGHHH!" I shrieked out. Fearlessly, Jerry grabbed my leg with one hand while trying to brush the giant slug off with the other, but in the end he had to yank the thing off, gripping and pulling at it frantically.

The others held onto one another, cowering at the far end of the room, horrified at the sight of me hobbling about bollock naked; not a pretty sight to witness when tripping out, I must admit.

Feeling shocked and violated I just stood there with my hands cupped over my private parts. It felt like I was going to slide into an epileptic fit or something. I looked around the room. Of course, Chong was unfazed by the whole performance and carried on skinning up while smiling to himself in his usual creepy way. The cunt.

"Bastard slugs, I fucking hate slugs, how the fuck did that slimy bastard get in my bath, eh?" I growled at my pals. No one reacted; all of them, with the exception of Chong, were still cowering in fear of the giant slug as it slowly made its way across the kitchen floor. The whole thing caught everyone off guard, even Tony who already knew about the slug.

Self-consciously I wandered back to the bathroom, shutting the door behind me and got back in my warm bath, trying to rationalise what had just taken place. I could hear them on the other side of the bathroom door bickering over who should get the giant slug out of the kitchen. Then all I heard was a weird squelching thump followed by a collective yelp of repugnance coming from my pals like something bad had occurred. I found out later on that night, what had actually happened was that Chong got up and stamped on it, and then he picked it up with his bare hands and slung it in the bin; the brutal fucker.

As I lay in the warm water my attention was quickly drawn to the sensation of my heart pumping - *buddum, buddum, buddum. I hope I don't have a heart attack and die in the bath like the late, great Jim Morrison,* I thought to myself, trying to visualise the scenario. However, after some more visualising I had to be honest about it, and admit that I probably looked more like a youthful Rab C. Nesbitt from the legendary BBC Scottish sitcom. The thought of dying in the bath became quite amusing for a few moments until I started fearing that I was possibly tempting fate - when taking into consideration that I had probably used up at least eight of those nine lives on my deathbed, sick with leukaemia as a teenager, and the sad fact that I wasn't a cat with nine lives!

The water was now cold so I got out of the bath quick sharp and then for some reason lay naked on the bathroom floor for moment wrapped in my bath towel, shivering. My head was throbbing with pleasurable agitation, things were getting pretty shambolic as all rationality seeped from my very being, too scared to move, lying there, terrified and shivering, watching the candles project flickers of light across the small room. Another wave of unrefined bliss shot up my spine, making my heart beat even harder. "Fuck, I could die here - maybe I've done too much?" I mumbled to myself in a state of total paranoia, scared for my life; wrapped in the soggy towel I could feel my body trembling like crazy.

The bathroom door crashed opened just missing the side of my head. This time Chong stepped nippily over me, making for the toilet, while at the same time rummaging about with the zip on his jeans. Then the discourteous slime ball proceeded to take a really long deep piss in the toilet. He looked over his left shoulder without any regard to what might be wrong with me. I stared back at him for a moment, while he was heedlessly splashing yellow junkie piss all over my floor and wall. "What's up, radgie-boy, you taking a whitey or something?"

"Nah, I thought that I was going to die for a moment there, until you crashed my scene," I responded sarcastically.

"Can I have your Peggy Pope ticket if you decide to go through with it?"

I just looked at the depraved fucker! Jumping up while at the same time struggling to keep the wet bath towel wrapped around my naked body, I headed out the bathroom door to my bedroom to get some time alone to sort my head out and get some clothes on. As I moseyed through, Jerry was head-banging to side two of the Peggy Pope album as the others watched on gurning like a bunch of malicious elves at a Halloween party; looking wide-eyed and - dare I say - a little frantic.

Whatever was in those Rhubarb and Custard capsules was some seriously heavy shit, I could feel it coming in surges of what can only be described as pure 'Ecstasy', however this was being randomly beaten back with surges of delirium; heaven and hell was entwined within the very nucleus of everything I focused my eyes and mind on. My head was an imploding bomb that was spitting streams of thought like splinters of shrapnel in every direction. I took another look at my gang of ghoulish pals as I fiddled with the bedroom door trying to get the damn thing to open. "I'm just getting some clothes on, boys, then I reckon we should head to the pub, eh?" I tried to sound enthusiastic, but in truth I was seriously dreading the night ahead. They all nodded back in silence, looking really confused, it was clear that no one had a fucking clue what I was talking about. *What a bunch of pure radges*; the thought brought me a few brief seconds of comfort, knowing whatever happened, I wasn't alone; I had my pals.

And, what about this ill-fated gang of cronies? Well ... Tony was training to be a counsellor by day, but by night he was usually drunk or off his tits on whatever he could lay his hands on, partying whenever possible, and spending money like there was no tomorrow. Yet, he always managed to somehow keep his shit together, regardless of the chaos going on within his personal life. I often wondered where he got all the money from, although it has to be said, Tony was never tight with his cash, he always got the rounds in and shared his drugs; a good lad, but mad as a brush.

As for the other three loons, well, Fergus I had known since we were little kids, he lived a few houses down from my mum and dad's house, he had loads of hang-ups about daft things like being terrified of dogs or scared of heights, you name it, he had some sort of weird psychological phobia or allergic reaction to it. Poor lad was teased silly throughout most of his childhood, but unfortunately he kept drawing attention to himself because of his uncontainable tantrums whenever he didn't get his own way. Fergus was prone to having proper hissy fits where he would slam doors or throw himself on the floor kicking and screaming like a spoilt brat, he was an easy target. Nevertheless, he could be really endearing at times, as well as being a good laugh.

Wallace was a bit of a lovable rascal who had a reputation for shagging older women, he loved grannies and mums, and was always getting himself unstuck because of his sleazy attitude towards the female race. There was a rumour flying around that he had caught herpes off of some old slag that he had shagged in the train toilets on his way to Inverness, one time. This never seemed to stop him, the dirty wee pervert, he always drew the attention of older ladies, and there never seemed to be any moral boundaries about what kind of age groups he would go for, the older they were, all the better as far as he was concerned.

As silly as it may sound, and because of the rumour, I was always careful that he got the same old Rangers F.C. mug when offering him a cup of tea whenever he was visiting, for fear of catching any horrid scabby viruses off the sleazy fucker. Unlucky for him, Thurso is a small town; news would spread like wildfire whenever he was caught sniffing around someone's gran, mum or auntie. We all knew his heart was in the right place, what could you do? He was a mate.

Then there was Cormag, who was actually a really nice guy who worked in the local butchers and was the most chilled out person I think I have ever known, which was probably because of him always being, and I mean *always* being stoned out of his mind. He was the only vegetarian butcher I had ever heard of or indeed known of and was very unconventional but in a very quiet, removed way; a lovely chap by all accounts. Also, he had the most amazing record collection I had ever seen, which took up two full floors of his house, which he lived alone in after inheriting it from his deceased parents who died within a three-year period of each other.

Aye, my pals were a right bunch of loons, but I knew deep down they were all fairly well-rounded lads, who had pretty much all been through the same grim shit that I myself had been put through as a result of living in a small isolated town where the north wind howled most of the time. I loved them, even though they were a bunch of sad freaks, far removed from my impeccable self, of course.

GIANT BROWN SLUG!

After spending some lost time talking to an invisible audience deep within my mashed-up head appraising the worthiness my pals, I randomly stepped over to the bedroom mirror and shook my head in an attempt to get my thoughts together. It was time to spruce up a bit and put a stop to this self-indulgent madness, so, after some effort I put my best clothes on, which instantly made me feel much, much better. Taking a deep breath, I finally gathered enough courage to open the bedroom door to face the façade of the here and now that was *probably* taking place in my living room. To my surprise I was actually starting to feel pretty good, if a little vague and wobbly. I opened the door. "Right, boys, are we heading out to the pub then?" I asked casually. Tony looked at his watch, appearing to be really surprised. "Fuck, is that the time already?"

All at once everyone was searching for jackets and shoes; a flap and fuss ensued as we all tried to get our shit together, except for Chong that is, he was busy making a spliff, casually spilling bits of tobacco and hash all over my coffee table, sniggering to himself. He gave me the creeps, the way he would laugh to himself like that.

Finally, after much fuss we all stepped out of the front door into the dark freezing night. Tony, Fergus, Wallace and Cormag were all looking slightly bemused, wide-eyed and visibly trying to keep their heads calm, considering that reality had now transformed into total weirdness. I took some comfort in reminding myself that I wasn't the only one going through this crazy shit. There were some more eruptions of anxious laughter, then for whatever reason we all fell silent and looked upwards in succession, even Chong managed to look up and ponder the magnitude of the Caithness skies.

We all gazed up in awe, tongue-tied until the freezing chill obliged us to gradually move on. I held back, taking in the silence for a few moments longer, there was a peculiar eerie, stillness as a rush of pleasure gushed deep within my chest again, and again. The stunning pitch-black textures lit up with all those shining diamonds, for a brief moment I felt there was love in this world and that things were going to be, okay. "Awesome!" I muttered, still gazing upwards. My neck was hurting; I spun around to make sure that the door was locked properly. *Yep, the door was locked.* Then, another quick check to make sure I still had my wallet and keys as well as our tickets for the gig. Thankfully, everything was okay. Then, there was need for one more quick door check, just to be really, really sure. *Yep, all's fine.*

By now the others were a small way ahead, their silhouettes bobbing up and down in the blue glimmer of the moon, this for some reason made me chuckle with delight. Then it dawned on me that plodding through the crunchy snow from my front garden was going to be a risky affair. Trying really hard not to slip on my arse, I carefully twinkle-toed it to the right onto the rough coastal path. I say coastal path, but really it was just a narrow dirt track that weaved through the darkness towards the orange glow of the town. The shoreline was situated to the right of the track, not a cliff edge as such, but enough of a drop to break a leg should you step the wrong way down the meandering rocks below.

Cautiously, I planned out a safe route, only to be stopped with a jolt as my eyes fixed on a most peculiar sight. "It's a rabbit's head?" I slurred to myself, spaced-out and baffled. Sure enough there was a decapitated rabbit's head sitting on the ice, right there before me. It looked really eerie, but strikingly beautiful too, maybe this was because of the peculiar shimmering glow reflecting off the ice that gave it a strange blue radiance, as its long wonderful whiskers twitched in the breeze, making it look like it was somehow, still alive? Stepping a bit closer, it occurred to me that it wasn't a wild rabbit; it was mostly black, but with a white stripe running down the centre of its nose and bottom part of its face. *This was a pet rabbit!*

I stared at it for a bit as a foreboding thought flashed into my head, that at any moment it was going to open its eyes to reveal empty black sockets. "Oi, check this out, boys!" impulsively, I shouted out to the others. They all stopped and looked back. "Seriously, come and check this out!" I insisted. I could hear their voices whining at the prospect of having to walk the hundred or so yards back to where I stood. First to reach me was Cormag, he stopped and looked at me for a moment wondering what was wrong; eventually the others caught up, still looking somewhat peeved at having to trek back over the icy cobblestones of snow. I stood pointing at the rabbit's head without saying a word to any of them, my mouth agape.

"Fucking hell, Danny's right, check this out, boys," Cormag reiterated as they all looked down and gathered around, gawping at the rabbit's head in silence for a few moments.

"What do you think happened to it?" asked Fergus.

"A cat, maybe?" replied Tony.

"Nah, that's not the work of a cat, how the fuck could a cat do that, ya fanny, that's the work of a human, you can tell by the way it has been done with one clean chop," replied Chong, with that condescending tone in his voice that suggested we were acting like a bunch of daft over-excited kids. "Aye, and I'll tell ye something else, that is most likely a sign that some fucker is going to die soon, voodoo or some sort of sanctified Satanism shit going on here, I reckon. Probably something to do with all those pet bunnies being decapitated, aye, are ye sure it's not you killing aw' these pet bunnies, Danny boy?"

"I couldn't eat a rabbit, let alone kill one," I responded jokingly. We all smirked at each other, trying to hide our discomfort at the grisly sight of the bodiless mammal. Chong was so full of shit, but none of us were ever brave enough to point it out to the twat, for fear of setting him off into one of his nasty outbursts, which always resulted in someone getting a kicking, or getting chibbed up, everyone was on their guard around the creep.

There was an unsettling hush as we all gazed some more at the poor wee thing. Then, without any sort of warning Wallace took a few steps backwards then booted the rabbit's head as hard as he could. It flew high into the air, tumbling in slow motion as the sheer revulsion of what he had just done washed across our insipid faces. I'll never forget the dull thudding sound it made as it hit the stone dyke wall then somehow tumbled perfectly upright in the frozen snow.

"Wallace, you sick fuck, what did you do that for?" Cormag screamed at him; clearly tripping out like a motherfucker. Wallace took a brave step forward, looked Cormag in the eyes with an evil sideways smirk on his face, "Cus I fuckingwell felt like it, alright, cunty-chops, and since when did you start caring about animals, you're a butcher, for fuck's sake!"

"Aye, but I am also an animal-loving vegetarian and there was no need to do that, have ye nae morals, ya loon?" Cormag snapped back through clenched teeth, clearly distressed and livid at this moronic behaviour. Wallace yelled back at him, "It's deid, ya numpty - DEID!"

There was a few seconds of silent tension, and then for some random reason everyone burst into a demented cackle. I struggled to hide my own feelings of disgust, sickened by this juvenile act, but eventually I joined in with the depraved cackling; not wanting my pals to think that I was some kind of soft lad or something. *Wallace is such a cock at times,* I thought to myself as I sauntered over to have one more look at the rabbit's head. How sad it looked; eyes still closed, sitting perfectly still in the moonlit snow once again.

The others walked off into the night, as I stood over the dead bunny. Uncontrollable gusts of gratification refrigerated me from the inside; yet, despite the chemical surge of counterfeit pleasure I felt sad. *How could anyone do such a cruel thing to a wee pet rabbit?* Snapping out of it with a shake of the head, I could feel my eyeballs drying up in the freezing air, I gave them a quick wipe with the back of my knuckles while trying to refocus, then I set off to catch up with the others.

The old ruins of Thurso Castle came into view as I laboured to catch a breath; the rushes were coming on strong. Then, all at once I was hit with the vibes of this wonderfully creepy archaic building to the left of me. I say castle, but really it was more of a roofless shell where the ravens and bats dwelled, although a more modern mansion house joins onto it via its defensive wall.

There was a real sense of antiquity mixed with a peculiar sombre grandeur to its silhouette, instantly reminding me of a Van Gogh painting that I once saw on a calendar as a child. *Funny the things you remember when you're off your face,* I thought as random associations rinsed through my brain like a river.

Normally I didn't pay too much attention to my surroundings, but tonight was different, all was enticing, everything had significance and shimmered with beauty. Gradually the narrow coastal path merged onto a wider path that meandered away from the small drop to the rocks below. To my left the path drew nearer to the north-facing wall of the castle and as I wandered on I passed the rusty remains of some old cannons, hopelessly pointing out to sea from where some old battlements once stood.

Finally, I caught up with the others as the sky gradually became contaminated with the dismal orange fog of the approaching streetlights of the town. Something I would never have noticed or even given a second thought to if I was in a sober state of mind. *Maybe this is how artists see the world?* I wondered. We walked on in silence up Sir Archibald Road past the coal-merchants and the Riverside Garage that looked out to where Thurso River meets the sea between the old harbour walls.

Drifting on we crossed over the footbridge and then past the British Legion, where we were met with the familiar sounds of bad karaoke bellowing out of a half-open doorway, some old guy stared us out as he smoked a fag. We took the shortcut up the back streets that led us into the centre of town.

It was a Saturday night and the town was buzzing with young folk heading out on the pish getting themselves tanked up for a wild night out in Thurso. As usual, there was a convoy of boy-racers spinning around in their zooped-up cars, aimlessly toot-tooting their horns at plump teenage girls. These girls would mostly hang around the shop doorways, chain-smoking and chewing gum; the skinnier ones looked more like pinch-faced ravens. The fat ones looked like plump clowns with self-harming issues, their glaring chubby faces coated with slabs of caked-on makeup gave me the shivers.

My mind felt crazed as we breezed through their thick plumes of smelly fag smoke blended with the toxic pong of bargain-basement perfume. Walking felt like the right thing to be doing, even though it was near impossible at times to know if I was walking or hovering.

The town was starting to look and feel more and more like some sort of fucked-up Narnia, full of disenchanted hobbits, bird-face bitches, as well as the odd nasty bastard looking for someone to pick a fight with. There was no doubt in my mind that we were all looking sketchy, loved-up, fucked up, and tripping-out all at once; it was a rabble of uncertainty laced with a menacing sense of not knowing what was coming next. Yet curiously, I felt totally self-assured with it.

There were disjointed conversations going on, but they never lasted very long since no one could finish a sentence with a full stop. Sentences would mutate into bizarre monologues of babble that always seemed to get lost in a trail of ruptured self-forgetting. There was an unexpected desire for beer; I needed to calm my head down, beer could do this, I was sure of it. The pub came into view, an oasis in this hellish Narnia.

The Poacher's Inn

We stepped into our favourite pub The Poacher's Inn, the place was half full; mostly with the same old intimidating alcoholics propping up the bar, except tonight they all appeared to be staring a bit more than they normally do, giving us all the pure evils from the moment we came through the door. Instinctively, common sense kicked in and we all tippy-toed by, pretending to be normal and of sane mind.

All of us stared at the floor avoiding any eye contact with the goons, that is, apart from Chong, who never seemed to give a flying fuck what anyone thought of him. He was like a bull in a china shop with megalomaniac issues, the idiot could have got us all lynched with that daft hippie coat and ridiculous hunting cap pulled over his smelly ginger dreadlocks making his sticky-out ears stick out even more than normal.

I noticed that some of the goons nodded at him in a rather evasive manner; even these psychos were a wee bit hesitant of the creep for fear of getting chibbed up. Aye, Chong was well known for his knife skills, and besides, he was one of the main suppliers in town, so generally they left him alone; he was of value to them. Anyway, Chong had contacts from down the line, aye, contacts that were connected to Inverness and Edinburgh, contacts that even the hard men of Thurso wouldn't be daft enough to mess with. Chong had protection, apparently. Personally I didn't buy into his bullshitting and the rumours about him. He was always going to be a chancer in my eyes. The twat.

As usual, The Dougie Blues Band, who had a residency at the pub were warming up on a small stage at the far end of the room, all dressed in candy pink bunny suits which I could only assume was part of some sort of fancy dress theme night, or some such nonsense or other.

I listened for a moment as they knocked out their usual mix of blues classics that erratically broke into jazzy wig-outs at every given opportunity. They were a great band and could really play their instruments, even though they were pished and stoned most of the time, which in my view was probably why they were so kick-ass tight. However, I've always had a sneaking suspicion that they were all secretly getting into jazz, which is no crime by the way.

Then again, who in their right mind wants to get pished listening to jazz? I mean, where's the tune and the beat in 'jazz' for fuck-sake? Ach, I've always had a bit of a tight-lipped loathing of anything 'jazzy'. Although, I have to concede that tonight the music was sounding really great, albeit a wee bit too ear-splittingly loud for my liking, and as usual the odd jazzy chord here and there that always irritated me, but only in the same way that horseradish makes me feel queasy.

Thoughts were rattling around my skull at supersonic speeds, yet there was a sense that everything was throbbing with meaning that translated somehow into patterns and textures of trancelike geometry oozing out of the threadbare carpet and scabby brown walls of the pub; intensely mesmerizing, and all at once. My mind was going into another meltdown episode as we all moved in a kind of unwieldy time-lapse, like we were stepping through a thick river of vibrant glue; movement made me feel listless and deflated. *This must be what it's like to be schizophrenic. What if I never come down? What if I stay like this?* Paranoia was getting the better of me as I struggled hard not to explode into a full-blown panic attack in front of the bunch of cold-blooded locals who had all been propping up the bar since lunchtime.

Without being able to resist the urge I took another quick look, they were still giving us the evils. Then without warning the internal monologue of my own voice started giving me a good verbal kicking. *For fucksake man, get a grip, ya daft cunt – this is hippie shite, ignore it, ignore it, you're going to be fine, just need to get a few beers down your neck.*

Conversations with myself rattled about in my skull like an iron ping-pong ball as I followed my pals' slow mosey through the pub. Again, I foolishly looked over at the scary men at the bar; sure enough, they were still gawking over at us like we'd done something wrong. The cunts.

Maybe I'm just being paranoid? One thing was certain; I had never ever been as high as this before and I don't mind admitting, I was now feeling really, really sketchy, too sketchy to be sitting amongst a bunch of local hard cases on a Saturday night. *What if my brain turns into a lump of spongy meat?* Worrying notions were coming fast and thick, but there was always that voice of cynical assurance; my voice, barking back at me, that *the brain is a lump of spongy meat, so there is nothing to actually worry about, ya daft bugger.* There seemed to be no let up from the perpetual monologue. *Lager – I needed lager – yes, yes lager! That will calm me down.* Neurotically ranting at myself over and over, *you just need to chill, have a drink and a wee sit down. I'll be fine, och, och . . .*

Awkwardness ensued, followed by a sense of relief as we all sat down after the long hellish trek through the pub. I could tell by all the worried looks on everyone's coupons that things had become seriously fucked up. Once again I got an impulsive fit of the giggles, which brought some comfort; I tried to calm my thoughts down and listen to the voice of common sense. *Don't panic!* It was nice to take the weight off my quivering legs for a bit; I felt like I was going to give birth to a litter of kittens; I needed to calm the fuck-down with all the crazy notions. My mind was racing and felt unsettled.

"Who's getting the fucking drinks in then?" demanded Chong with a psychotic sneer; he was obviously feeling the tension of the situation, even though the tetchy fucker was the only one among us who wasn't actually tripping out; Chong wasn't too fond of psychedelics. Even the ecstasy, and all the other unpleasant drugs he had shot up his nose and into his veins, didn't seem to cheer the miserable arsehole up. I caught Tony secretly rolling his eyes while asking everyone what they wanted to drink, and then courageously he headed for the bar, Fergus followed him, but you could see that they weren't right. *Brave!* I thought.

We sat in silence, avoiding any eye contact with each other, pretending to watch the band. *I wonder what the bunny suits are about?* I pondered quietly to myself in a rare moment of calmness. Gazing back over at Tony I couldn't help noticing how jittery he was acting at the bar, fidgeting like crazy to find his wallet. Of course, this turned into a rather melodramatic performance as he patted all over his body looking really uncomfortable, but finally digging it out of his shirt pocket, thanks to the barman spotting it for him. By the time he and Fergus had squeezed back through the crowded bar area with the trays of drinks you could see that they were both rattled, and oblivious to the lager spillage that dripped from the plastic trays onto the floor. *How beautiful those liquid puddles are,* I thought as they reflected mini rainbows from the flashing lights of the fruit machine.

Massive waves of euphoria zipped through my spine again, and again, but this time it was way more full on, making my jaw clench in a very pleasing manner. I noticed that all of us were at it, gurning like a bunch of billy goats chewing on the cud. As soon as I took a sip of lager my mood changed, feeling a bit miffed to find that it still had that delicate crispy effect. I took another sip, and then another, trying to ignore the strange crispy texture of the lager. *Okay, so I am sat at a table with a bunch of blissed-out furry fuckers drinking crispy lager? Hoe hum.* I surrendered to the moment.

As the evening pressed on we drank pints and pints of lager, but it was having little effect on us as far as I could see, but thankfully the furry thing had worn off and the mood had lightened up, a wee bit. Actually I was starting to feel pretty good even if I was completely dumbstruck. Jerry and Chong kept sneaking off to the bogs, I assumed to smoke hash pipes; this was a normal ritual in The Poacher's Inn. The bar staff and manager of the place kindly turned a blind eye to such shenanigans, they weren't too bothered so long as everyone was spending money at the bar and no one was shooting smack in the cubicles. Hash smoking was tolerated, so long as it was kept out of sight and no dealing was going down.

I watched Jerry and Chong push their way through the now crowded bar towards the toilets for the third time, I needed to go for a slash and couldn't be arsed to forge my own path, it was easier to follow Chong as he forced his way through. Luckily, I slipped into a cubicle without the pair of them even noticing me. I could tell they were up to something, but I couldn't quite make out their mutterings as my powers of concentration drifted here and there. I was way too out of it to focus anymore. *Bah,* I thought, swaying about like I was on a boat out in rough seas.

After another mind-blowingly long pee I became ever so slightly mesmerized by an oily stain on the wall directly in front of me as it throbbed and pulsated into the shape of a witch's face, I had to look away for fear of it coming to life and speaking to me. I let out an unhinged cackle. *The night has only just started!* I thought as I felt my heart pounding in my rib cage, but this time with a regularity that I felt very comfortable with. The wooziness seemed to have eased off a little; finally I was starting to feel a wee bit of self-control coming back to me.

My focus was quickly drawn back to Chong and Jerry in the next cubicle as they muttered away to each other, but I was too disorientated to really comprehend what they were banging on about, and then I heard Jerry thanking him for something, and then a door banged open. I assumed they had gone back up the steps into the pub. As I looked back at the stain on the wall, it started to swell and throb, morphing back into the face of the old hag again.

I needed to gather my thoughts and try and enjoy this, after all, isn't that what it was supposed to be all about? Still, if I was truly honest about the situation it was more like a house of horrors mashing-up my skull. I gave my dick another shake and tucked it back in while swaying about trying to pull the fly of my trousers up, once that was sorted I turned to the door behind me. I start fidgeting like crazy to get the lock of the cubicle undone and then without warning I pulled the door open, making a deafening bang.

The first thing I see is Chong leaning against the wall by the hand dryer, I tried to avoid eye contact with the tosser, but he lured me over with an nod. He had that crazed glint in his eye where you weren't too sure what the nasty fucker was going to do next. As he drew me even nearer to where he was stood I couldn't help noticing a white amphetamine crystal stuck to a small ball of snot that clung to a ginger hair poking out of his long hooked nose.

He swayed back and forth for a moment then proceeded to spray spit all over my face with every word that came from his vile mouth as his rotten teeth took on the form of tombstones. His breath stunk like someone had taken a shit in his mouth, the smell made me heave as I tried to hide my repugnance from the filthy fuckwit. The last thing I needed right now was for him to take offence and turn on me. However, it didn't take long to realise that he was going to turn nasty anyway; there wasn't much I could do about it apart from accept my punishment and take it like a man.

"Aye, so, Danny boy, what exactly did ye mean by calling me a philistine earlier on?" At first I stared blankly at the prick, struggling to understand what the hell he was banging on about. As far as I could remember I hadn't at any point said he was a philistine. There was no fucking way - I wouldn't dare say such a thing out aloud for fear of having to pluck my teeth out of my arse as a direct result of getting my heid stomped on. My mind raced for answers, then it struck me like a clout to the head. *I have only ever had the thought that he was a philistine! Maybe he can read my mind after all?* "Eh? I don't have a clue what you're going on about; I didn't call you a philistine, that's not even a phrase I'm familiar with, mate."

"Aye ye did, radgie-boy!" He gave me one of his creepy smirks. I gave him a puzzled look as I mentally braced myself, guessing that he was going to grab me by the hair and smash my face off of the sink that I was leaning up against. Daringly, I tried to defend myself. "That's not even a word I would use, let alone understand, what is a philistine anyway?"

He looked deep into my eyes and gave me another creepy smirk; I smirked back at him, letting out a nervous whimper. "Aye ye did, Danny! Aye, watch yourself, Danny boy, because for all you know I may have been sent to ruin your day."

I felt violated as more of his rancid spit sprayed all over my face, once again. I shrugged my shoulders back at him, feeling way too scared to think or say anything else on the off chance the creep really did have telepathic powers. He gave me a rough man-slap on the side of my face and pointed his finger at my nose. I tittered back at him nervously, waiting for the vicious outburst to ensue. But weirdly, he unceremoniously changed the subject and started pestering me to eat a lump of hash or something along those lines, at least that's what I thought he was saying. It was hard to hear him over the rabble of live music coming from upstairs.

"Here's a wee bit of compensation for forgetting to get your hash order in, ya wee *philistine*." I looked at the lump of hash in his hand and thought, *what the fuck, if it's going for free and it keeps this psycho from nutting me in the face - I mean, what else can I do but go along with the fanny? This fucker is a fully-fledged psychopath for Christ-sake!* So, with a combination of out and out foolishness mixed with genuine fear, I quickly chucked the hash into my gob to prevent the psycho from turning again and beating the shite out of me. Chong gave me another weighty tap on the side of my face then pointed his finger again, and then he let out a raspy laugh, consequently spraying more spit in my face.

Carefully, I pulled away from the crazy scumbag and headed back upstairs, taking a brief look over my shoulder to make sure he wasn't following me, but to my relief he had nipped back into a cubicle, locking the door behind him. It was hard to put my finger on it but there was some bad juju going down with Chong, he was so erratic, it was only a matter of time before the fucker was actually going to kill someone; I could sense it. We needed to shake rid of him or our night would be doomed!

The hash tasted rank as it started to dissolve under my tongue. As quick as I could I gently pressed my way through the crowd back to where my pals were all sat. Without any further ado I washed the hash down with the dregs of my pint, not really thinking about the consequences of my actions, all I was concerned about was getting the nasty taste out of my mouth. Then I spent at least twenty minutes or so sitting in silence, trying really hard not to be sick in front of my pals, and I was fucked if I was going to make it all the way back to the toilets again. Anyway, my legs were not working anymore. Jerry leaned over and shouted in my ear. "Are you okay, mate?"

I looked back at him for a moment, and then shouted in his ear over the loud music, "Aye, I think so, Chong just gave me a lump of hash, for free."

Jerry looked at me for a moment. "Where is it?" he asked.

"Um, I ate it," I answered.

"How much did you eat?" he snapped sharply.

"Um, a bit about the size of my thumbnail, I guess?" I mumbled back at him.

"Danny, you plonker, that wasn't just any old bit of hash, dude, that was 'Sputnik' which is top quality Moroccan hash; it's fucking dynamite, you crazy fool!"

"Oops," I replied, feeling goofy as fuck until another wave of queasiness washed over me. Jerry gave me one of his kooky grins; I could see he was speechless. It occurred to me that I might have consumed a dangerous cocktail of drugs; I quickly shook the thought off, but the worry kept welling up in me. Paranoia surged through me; moments became days, going on for ages and ages, and ages.

My mood changed again and then again as the music slowly seeped into my brain, gently lifting me from my inner hell. I felt indestructible, but still a little queasy. Jolts of pleasure zipped up and down my spine, again and again. *Just a wee wobble, Danny, nae bother*, I reassured myself as I sensed the blood pumping through my veins, surely confirmation that all was well. *Maybe I wasn't going to croak after all; maybe I'm actually going to have a great time!* I concluded, trying to be a bit more light-hearted about the situation in hand. My eyes felt really heavy as I tried to stop them rolling in their sockets. I clung to my chair for dear life; bliss and torment all in one fell swoop. *Ding-dang-fucking-DOO!* I thought, while sensing myself grinning erratically. I felt ace.

My head started nodding to the music as the Dougie Blues Band broke into some jazzy number, which I must admit was sounding astoundingly good to my ears, like I say, I don't normally like jazz, but tonight it exploded out of the cheap PA system like liquid gold - all at once I 'got' what jazz music was all about, and to my astonishment I started really getting into it, and I mean - really - getting into it!

Like bad weather, Chong returned to the table and sat in the chair next to me, I noticed his eyes were rolling into the back of their sockets. *That'll be the skag kicking in*, I thought while looking at his septic arms all covered in nasty syringe wounds. Then in a particularly creepy manner the fucker looked straight into my eyes as if he'd heard my thoughts.

I felt uneasy as he reached over for his glass and proceeded to neck half of a pint in one greedy gulp, pausing for a quick breather, then continued to gulp the rest of the pint down. There was a small pause and for a split second I really thought he was going to puke everywhere but instead he just slammed the empty glass on the table, and then he wiped the dribbles from his mouth with the back of his hand. His lack of manners made me shudder with repugnance as I noticed he still had the amphetamine crystal stuck to the small ball of snot that still clung to the horrid ginger hair poking out of his hooky nose.

For no reason whatsoever he started slagging off the band by standing up doing the wanker sign then giving the middle finger, while gurning in an unsettling manner. You could tell by looking at the twat that he was on some really heavy shit; his eyes looked crazed as his screwball behaviour started to draw the attention from the bar staff, but even they were reluctant to deal with him; they had seen this all before. Chong had been banned from The Poacher's Inn many, many times, but for some reason they always seemed to let the weasel back in.

Naturally, we all tried to act like we weren't with the maniac, all of us pretending to watch the band while supping our pints as if he weren't there. Dougie looked directly over from the stage, giving Chong the evils, but looking really comical in his candy pink bunny suit. Chong gave him another wanker sign then slumped back onto his chair, nearly falling backwards onto his arse.

Tony had kindly splashed out and bought everyone another round of drinks; everyone showed their appreciation as

The Poacher's Inn

Cormag and Jerry reached over to help him with the large tray of drinks. Of course, there were no offers of gratitude coming from Chong; he was too busy acting like a fucking nutcase, ranting some sort of spiteful bile about how shit the band was. I could tell the fucker was going to kick off as he made everyone at the table feel more and more uncomfortable. The tray in Tony's hand wobbled as he carefully placed the last pint on the table in front of Chong, which he knocked back in another few greedy gulps. *This guy's a fiend; surely it isn't normal for someone to drink like that?* I watched him wipe the dribbles and snot from his mouth and nose with the sleeve of his saggy old knitted jumper. I looked away, sickened by the very sight of him.

The pub was getting pretty busy now and people were trying to squeeze their way through to the bar. Reaching forward to pick up my pint, I felt a firm shove from behind my seat, making me lose balance and spill my lager all over Chong's putrid old coat that was slung over the arm of his chair next to me. Luckily for me, Chong saw what happened, so at least he knew it wasn't my fault.

We watched on as the anger erupted from his face while he stretched his coat over my lap, trying to brush the beer drips off it, soaking me in the process. *Oh-fuck, here we go!* Chong started ranting and raving about what he was going to do to the guy who had unwittingly bumped into the back of my chair. Bravely, I tried to reason with the crazed fuckwit, "Come on now, mate, it was an accident, the guy didn't mean it, in fact he didn't even see it!"

Of course, he totally ignored my pleas as he looked around the pub, trying to pick out the guy who hadn't even noticed the incident and was now lost in the crowd of people who were all watching the band doing their jazzy wig-outs.

"I'm going to put this pint glass in pretty-boy's face and stamp on the cunt's throat and watch him squeal for his mammy!" he hissed at us all like a devil as his horrible spit sprayed all over the table. We all took turns trying to reason with him, knowing full well he meant what he was saying; we all knew what was coming next.

True to form, the daft prick got louder and louder, stirring himself into another one of his psychopathic episodes. I could see the veins at the side of his ugly ginger head get fatter and fatter as the rage intensified within him, and then erratically he stood up, trying to spot his unsuspecting target.

Then he was off, shoving his way through the crowd to get at the lad who was now standing with a girl by one of the speakers at the far side of the stage. Chong lurched headlong through the crowd, but in his blundering haste he lost his balance, falling awkwardly and backwards onto the small stage, causing one of Dougie's guitars to tilt off its stand, making it crash to the floor. He got himself back up, totally oblivious of the chaos he was causing. A bizarre chain of events ensued.

Dougie had clocked Chong's shenanigans from the get-go, he stopped playing mid-song; his band being professionals played on, but were noticeably raising eyebrows and shaking their heads at each other, wondering what the hell Dougie was doing. All of us watched on from the safety of our table as Dougie, looking slightly ridiculous in his candy pink bunny onesie took his guitar off, carefully placing it in its stand, and then he stepped off the stage shaking his head.

Calmly and politely he wove his way through the audience, quickly catching up with Chong who was still totally unaware and preoccupied with shoving people out of his way. Dougie tapped him on the shoulder and as Chong turned around with a crazed look on his face, Dougie knocked him clean out

The Poacher's Inn

with a single head-butt to the nose. For a moment Dougie stood over Chong, fists clenched, waiting for him to get back up. Thankfully, Chong didn't get back up. Dougie turned and walked back through the mob of punters who were all now looking pretty stunned and gathering around Chong, who was still out cold.

Dougie was as cool as ice about the whole matter and picked up the knocked-over guitar and put it back in its stand, and then he stepped on the stage and picked up his other guitar and carried on with the song. The rest of the band was in hysterics as Dougie started crooning with a deep tender voice. There was a roar of support from the locals standing at the bar, who were well impressed. *Just another night out at The Poacher's Inn and it couldn't have happened to a nicer chap!* I chuckled to myself.

Eventually the barman and another big guy came over to our table and asked if Chong was with us in a very accusing manner. Completely terrified, we shook our heads as if we had nothing to do with it. I handed Chong's smelly coat over to the barman and explained that we didn't see what had happened and that he wasn't really part of our group, making out that he was being an intimidating pest that we couldn't get rid of. Thankfully he bought my story and decided not to chuck us all out. Chong was dragged out of the pub by the scruff and bundled out of the front doors.

We watched on in silence as he pathetically bawled empty threats at the two heavies who were trying really hard to avoid any contact with his horrible junkie blood. Even from inside the deafening pub you could hear the sound of the weasel's pleas echoing over the music.

Looking back over at the stage I could see people were gathering round to watch the band. I couldn't help staring as the townies and their raven-faced girlfriends bopped about to the music, unaware that they were dancing and smearing all of Chong's blood into the shabby old carpet. *If only they knew*, I thought as the red droplets splashed in slow motion all over the pretty legs of the girls in their miniskirts. *Hard to believe that so much blood could come from such a small cut.*

We looked at each other, shaking our heads in disbelief. But, just as we thought that was the end of it, like something out of a nightmare Chong appeared outside the window behind the stage, pressing his ruptured face up against the glass, furiously screaming some sort of futile bile at Dougie, who had his back turned to him, preoccupied with performing another awesome guitar solo.

The fear rose in me as I watched Chong open his mouth in a quick snapping action that turned into a weird juddering of his jaw, showing off his freaky oversized buckteeth as blood and snot smeared down the window. All of a sudden the big guy from the bar was up on the stage next to the drummer, lunging forward to the inside of the window pointing his finger at Chong, mouthing a final threat that couldn't be heard because of the music, but probably equated to something along the lines of: MOVE ON, CUNT, BEFORE I STOVE YER FUCKING HEID IN!

Chong was gone, leaving only two blood-smeared handprints on the outside of the window. Even he knew better than to mess around with the thugs that ran The Poacher's Inn. He was lucky to get off with just a broken nose, the stupid twat. Anyway, we were all thankful to be rid of the prick, fucking putting everyone on a downer and spoiling our trip. It was like he was sent to fuck up our night the way he randomly showed up at my door like that; he gave me the pure heebie-jeebies.

Everyone sat round the table gave a sigh of relief as the mood picked up a notch. I looked back over at the big guy from the bar, who was now stood by the door on the off chance that Chong would try to sneak back in, but you could tell he didn't really give a shit as he started banging his fat head to the music. I feel kind of ashamed to admit it, but this was all perfectly normal for a Saturday night in The Poacher's Inn, Chong would no doubt be barred again, surprise, surprise.

The music stopped for a bit and the band stepped off the stage making their way toward the bar, in their daft bunny onesies. I was spacing out like a don't-know-what, watching Bandy-pup, Munchy-Fudge, Burk and Evil-Devil Timmy Dooley, drunk as skunks, goading each other to have their heads shaved for charity by Gay-Billy, the only male hairstylist in town. In a flash a space was cleared and a chair pulled up. Billy started to shave Bandy-pup's hair off whilst his mates staggered about, chanting him on and clapping their hands.

The rest of the alkies at the bar rolled their eyes at each other then went back to watching the Celtic vs Rangers highlights on a big TV that had the volume turned down. Apart from the candy pink bunnies, they all looked like fat gargoyles to me as I watched them all chuffing away on fags, casually filling the place up with toxic smoke.

I love this pub! I thought while bursting into uncontainable hysterics. The candy pink bunnies walked back to the stage, picked up their instruments and started playing *Whole Lotta Love* by Led Zeppelin, a song I normally hated, but tonight it sounded totally awesome. Looking over again at my mates, we weren't saying much, but we all knew that we didn't need to. We were a fucking team.

All of us smiling and rocking our heads to the music, giving each other discerning looks tinged with utter bewilderment, with the exception of Jerry that is, he was in his own little world preoccupied with sticking his finger up his nose. He kept digging deeper and deeper with his finger; the others were busy getting into the band and weren't paying much attention to what he was doing, but slyly I watched on; I couldn't help it. Eventually he pulled this long slither of snot out of his nose and when I say long, I mean - it was long! Then radgie-boy secretly wipes it under the table. *Eww - you filthy fucker.* He noticed that I had caught him out then he leaned over the table. "You are aware of the rules of snot, aren't you, Danny?" he asked in his posh accent.

"What the fuck are you talking about, ya nutcase? And by the way, I seen what you just did with that snotter there, ya filthy fecker!" I slurred back at him.

"Nah, mate, I'm playing within the rules of snot!"

I looked back at him, confused, "The rules of snot?"

He nodded back at me, smiling, "Yeah, the rules of snot! Always flick or wipe a morsel with the understanding that you are symbolically marking your territory, which is within the genetic makeup of all males, animal or human. Also, see it as a means of clearing out all the dark potholes in your nose."

"You winding me up?" I replied.

He smiled back at me like I was the mad fucker, "Also, there is the telepathic code of conduct that after a day or two spiders will come and recycle the (dried) snot by using it as bait to draw bugs into their webs!" I looked back at him, wondering if he had actually gone insane. He looked at me while touching the side of his nose, silently mouthing the word:

snot. *Crazy fucker!* I concluded to myself, not quite understanding what had just happened there.

Later on, once all our nerves had been soothed with a little help of some whiskey, we made a pact to stick together at all costs and to make an effort to get to the gig earlier, rather than be late. It felt great to bond with my pals like this as we agreed to try our best to watch out for each other, seeing as the mood could drop like a house of cards due to our tripped-out state. As Tony rightly pointed out - "Aye, it's not often you get gigs of this calibre in Thurso; let's make the most of it!"

The decision was made to drink up and make our way out of the jam-packed pub. Feeling much better after a few bevvies, we were ready to hit the second part of our journey when we all noticed the trail of smeared blood that Chong had left on the snow-covered path outside by the doorway of the pub. No matter which way I looked at it, I just couldn't feel any empathy for the twat. Carefully, I stepped around the messy puddles of blood, worried that I might get it on my new trainers. *Funny, how karma always sorts an evil cunt out.* I told myself as a wicked smirk reached across my face.

Drugs and Aliens

It was snowing heavily again as me and my pals marched further up through the back streets to get to the outskirts of town, taking us out beyond the police station then eventually out by the campsite, which was not too far from where The Old Bay Inn was situated. The wind developed into a gale, whooshing around us, freezing our hands and faces to the point where it squeezed every bit of warmth from our skinny bodies.

My forehead stung as a throbbing pain pounded above my eyebrows. Tony stopped and appeared to be waiting for me to catch up; I could feel him gawking at me as he laughed out aloud in a crazed deranged cackle. "I have just the thing to sort you out, Danny boy." Digging around in his pocket he pulled out a wrap of white powder, which turned out to be speed he had bought off of Chong earlier on, around the time that I was having a panic attack in the bath. He offered me the wrap, but I decided to be cautious and only had a few wee dabs while trying really hard not to drop it with my freezing hands or indeed, let the wind blow it away. Tony gave me a crafty wink then had a few dabs himself as the wind threatened to blow it out of his shivering grip. Within seconds I was rushing and gurning like a motherfucker again;

the speed totally lit me up. "Just the ticket!" I chuckled to myself.

With a fresh surge of energy we ran to catch up with the other boys, who were hunched up walking into the increasing blizzard at an impressive pace. Once we had caught up with them they were debating whose round it was and who was feeling brave enough to go to the bar first, seeing as we were all tripping out like Albert Hoffman's long lost bastard sons.

"I'll go to the bar, but you'll all have to chip in with the cash, because I'm a bit skint after giving Chong that tenner earlier on!" I knew as soon as I made this offer I was somehow going to deeply regret it. We eventually made it to The Old Bay Inn; however, it took another twenty minutes or so of hanging around in the car park freezing to death before we could convince Fergus that he wasn't about to be killed by blood sucking Greys. Then it took another twenty minutes or so to convince the radge that The Old Bay Inn wasn't a mother ship full of little alien doctors waiting to stick drills up his arse or push long pins into his stretched eyeballs.

Normally I would laugh my head off at such rubbish, but this was becoming quite distressing to witness, he was having a proper melt down in front of us all. The fecker even started worrying about those cunts the Banana Splits possibly being at the gig, I quickly tried to dismiss the idea, they scared me much more than any *Grey* ever could.

Thankfully, after a few dabs of Tony's speed Fergus finally agreed to go in, which was a good job because he was seriously beginning to drag us all into his horrifying delusion with him. We were all starting to debate among ourselves if it was actually a hotel, or like Fergus had suggested, a mother ship full of alien doctors pretending to be locals. Collectively our minds raced with conspiracy, but common sense prevailed and we bravely stepped through the main doors of the building, apprehension noticeably etched across our spaced-out faces as we handed our tickets to the bouncer while trying really hard to act normal in front of the weird bar staff that moved like insects behind the bar.

Wallace staggered into a stool and started apologising to it, convinced he had knocked over a dwarf. I tussled with the zip on my coat, struggling to get my frozen hands to work as I tried to explain to him that it was only a stool, and to stop acting like a crazy man. The others were all looking vague as fuck, but thankfully had enough self-control to scuttle over to a rather welcoming candlelit table that was placed near the empty stage.

There was a stern voice from the other side of the bar. "What would ye like, hen?" I looked up and sure as fuck, there was this old barman staring at me, except he wasn't human, no, he was a reptilian-grey hybrid pretending to be human. I could tell this by the plastic bunny ears that were badly stuck to his large oval-shaped head.

"Um, um, six pints of lager please, mate," I responded tentatively. He started pouring pints, while staring suspiciously over at Wallace who was still apologising to the barstool. I drew back for a moment, seriously trying to gather my thoughts, trying to talk myself out of running away from the joint, trying desperately to weigh up in my head if in fact Fergus may have been right after all. *Maybe this was a fucking trap! Maybe we were going to get drills put up our arses! Maybe we were just food to those Nazi-Grey fuckers?*

Wallace interrupted my relapse by tapping me on the shoulder; I jumped and dropped all the coins onto the floor. Wallace started laughing uncontrollably as I scrambled around trying to pick the coins up, which were rolling off in every direction in a slow *hellish* motion. Somehow, I managed to stay calm and eventually gathered together all the coinage, putting it back on the bar while trying really hard to concentrate on counting it up again.

The Grey looked at me silently, assessing my sketchy performance, and for a moment I really feared that he was going to grab me by the throat and bite a chunk out of my face, then slurp all the blood from me with his long, black forked tongue. In my mind's eye I visualised him disposing of my empty carcass in the industrial sized wheelie-bins out at the far end of the car park. *Aye, I've read all about what those Grey alien radges do to us humans; we're just fucking livestock to them and earth is really just an experiment that got way out of control, this is common knowledge!* My mind was made up in a second!

"That'll be sixteen pounds eighty, please," he hissed at me in a nippy way, looking like a right prat with those plastic bunny ears stretched to the max across his grey bulbous head. I pushed the pile of coins and five pound notes towards him, "That should be right, mate, sorry about all the loose change."

"Nae bother," he snapped, then this dark blue fork-shaped tongue flicked out of his tiny mouth at lightning speed, licking the side of his warty face as he counted out the money at an uncanny speed. *Holy Christ, their tongues are blue?* At this stage I was seriously considering getting the hell out of the place, but then I was faced with a distracting predicament as I reached for the tray of lagers. Immediately I realised that there was no way that I was ever going to be able to carry that lot across the dance floor and past the stage area without slipping on my arse and spilling it all. "Oi, cunt-chops, help me with the beers!" Wallace was pissing himself laughing so much; tears were now streaming down his face, I looked at him for a moment, reeling with pent-up agitation, "What's so funny?"

"Fergus was spot on, this place is full of aliens, and what's all this business with the silly bunny ears?" he responded with a sudden deadpan look on his face.

"Keep your voice down, man, they could turn on us, shush!" I pleaded, quickly spotting the barman staring over at us again. Cautiously we scuttled over to where the others were all sat. Cormag got up and helped me with the pints then took me aside and had a quiet word in my ear, "Danny, don't mention that the staff in here are Greys for fuck-sake!"

"BUT THEY ARE!" I screeched back at him as the worry took hold.

"Look, man, we are all going to miss the gig if Fergus finds out that they really are Greys, he thinks it's just the drugs messing with his heid."

I looked over at Fergus, who was staring at the floor mumbling to himself, while Jerry tried to convince him that he was okay and that there was nothing to be worried about. Cormag grabbed me by the arm and said in a comforting voice, "these alien gadgies seem to be friendly enough, let's not panic and hang around for the gig, yeah?"

"Okay, fair enough, let's stay for the gig, sure," then I looked him in the eye and posed the question, "so, are you saying that it isn't the drugs, by the way?"

Cormag smiled at me for a moment, and then shrugged his shoulders. I let out a nervous chuckle, and then we shook hands on it, as we both sat down at the table with the others. I reached over and took a sip of my pint; the gentle crispy texture of the lager hit the back of my throat, triggering the anxiety about my teeth all over again. Letting out a deep sigh I tried to comprehend the craziness going on, but at that very moment and out of nowhere a shooting pain hit my nether regions like I was being gently poked up the arse with a blunt knitting needle. After a while the jabbing pain gathered momentum, when it started dawning on me that I wasn't feeling very well. A heavy wooziness took hold, but this time it was different. *Heh, maybe it is just the drugs after all?* I reasoned with myself.

"You okay, Danny? You've gone a funny yellow colour, are you going to puke?" questioned Jerry, who was looking a bit concerned for me while at the same time discreetly moving out of range, on the off chance I was going to projectile vomit everywhere. I looked over at him as another stab of pain shot up me, making me feel like I needed to take a shit - urgently! "I'm not sure, mate, I'm feeling a bit dodgy actually, where's the bogs? My heid is all over the place, I can't remember where anything is anymore." Before he could raise his arm to point me in the right direction I was off in an agitated flap, while trying really hard to hide my internal misery as much as possible as I rushed past the reptilian barman. I could sense the sneaky fucker's almond-shaped eyes on me again as I looked about for the toilets.

Pure torment set in as I envisaged myself exploding shit all over the dance floor if I didn't find a fucking toilet quickly. Spotting the toilet sign, I made a dash toward the door, thrusting myself through it and straight into the nearest cubicle, while anxiously fumbling with my belt trying to get my trousers off before I shit myself. Thankfully, the toilet seat appeared to be semi-clean as I whipped my jeans down to my ankles and parked my bum on the freezing cold plastic seat.

The shits squirted out of my bum like heavy lumps of porridge being hurled at force from a large wooden spoon. There was a brief moment of relief as the inner pain eased a little, then it started brewing up in my nether regions once more, only to explode out of my arse again and again, and again making a loud farting squelch that hit the toilet pan with a repulsive splat. I felt sick. Beads of sweat were running down my face.

I started to get really scared that my liver was going to drop out of my arse and I was doomed to die on the toilet seat just like Elvis did, except I wasn't fat, but then again, I wasn't Elvis. No, I was just some drugged-up loser, dying in a public toilet of my choice. *What a rubbish way to go,* I thought to myself as my arse fired out another round of Satan's porridge. I surrendered to the pandemonium going on within me and the urge to live started to fade like a dream, then all I could sense was a black nothingness, you know that place we all wander to, when there is no hope left.

Who the fuck is Alan Watts?

It was completely fucked up and weird, I wasn't attached to my body anymore and the pain was gone. *Am I dead?* I asked myself as a strange calmness rippled through me. My body was gone; I had turned into an orb of bright light. Oddly enough, I was okay with it; I had been here once before when I was a teenager suffering from leukaemia trapped within the gloomy geriatric wards of Glasgow Royal Infirmary. By the time I was finally given a bed in the specialist cancer ward I had been in hospital for well over a year. Then, rather unexpectedly, there was a glimmer of hope that I was actually getting better, and that there was a reasonable chance that I was going to possibly live.

However, I developed complications from a tooth infection as a result of eating too much chocolate. The reason I had eaten so much chocolate was because it was Easter, which meant Easter eggs, and chocolate Easter bunnies - lots of them! You see, I had been starved of chocolate, no dairy products were allowed for nearly a whole year; my immune system was too low to deal with it as a result of heavy doses of chemotherapy. That, and the fact that one of the other side effects of chemo is that it kills off any ability to taste food, and because of my sudden recovery this was the first time in ages that I could actually taste chocolate again. This was a massively big deal for me - I love chocolate!

Alas, I had to have all my upper front teeth removed in an emergency operation to drain the puss from a massive abscess that had developed in my mouth overnight, it swelled up so much that it made me look like the Elephant Man. It was so awful to see my face like that. Pulling all my top teeth out was the only way the physicians could stop the poison from reaching my brain, seeing as I still had a frail immune system that couldn't fight the infection; it was the only option. I'm pretty sure I died for a little while on that operating table, or at least came very close to death. You know, gone but not gone.

This was a very similar sensation and with that unmistakable feeling of being detached from everything that involved my life as Danny Texas, kind of like saying goodbye to yourself, but without words. Immediately, I recognised that deep sense of deliverance combined with bursts of heart-breaking disappointment, as I found myself peering back down at the pathetic sight of my body slumped on the toilet seat while beads of sweat rolled down my pale face that was squashed against the cubicle wall.

All of a sudden there was a sense of being lured away by a higher force, a force that was beyond any grasp of comprehension, tugging gently within. Looking upwards, I could just make out a swirling void with a small spec of light at the end of it. *This must be what it's like to be dead then? This must be the light at the end of the tunnel that everyone bangs on about. Heh, I must be dead?* I knew this was it, then, there was a voice; but this time it wasn't my voice.

"Danny, I don't have an awful lot of time, dear chap, my name is Alan Watts, you've probably heard about me. No?

Oh well, that's all by the by. Anyway, I have been sent to warn you about the curse, but you're going to be okay, your uncle Hamish has sent a guardian who will decapitate the heads of those who spit the blood and cast the spell. Hamish is with me now, but he is forbidden to speak to you because of the laws of karmic assessment and corporeal reassignment." There was another pause, and then the voice of Alan spoke again. "He tells me that he is angry with you for drinking the brew!"

But Uncle Hamish is dead, I thought, while trying to understand what was happening and then the voice spoke again . . . "Once you realise that this is it, it's kind of like the tumour of misconception has been vaporised and the smoke screen is finally lifted; all your inner fears of passing over dissolve. Only then, will you realise that you have always been, and you will always be, you are infinite and perpetual. Birth, sex, death, then rebirth over and over again, that's all we are, but fear not, for you will always be 'YOU!' - do you hear me, lad? Only when you break free from the eternal wheel will you be truly free to move on, this may never happen in some cases of course, due to what is known as: *karmic impairment.*" Another short pause ensued, and then the voice spoke again. "Now, Danny, I will grant you a quick review of the future."

There was a flash of light, but when I looked closer I realised it wasn't a light at all, it was loads and loads of images of me, like watching a weird movie in fast motion playing out a sort of mini review of my future life. But the really weird thing about it was, that I could feel all the raw emotion of what I was observing. Somehow, I sense that I am in the company of a new girlfriend, we run away to Aberdeen, mainly because she was attending college there; taking her Highers in art. Falling head over heels with this unnamed girl was easy; she appears to be a quiet hippie girl, who seems happy to sit around all day smoking pot. This was my kind of girl, unlike Alison who detested the fact that I smoked pot and nagged me about constantly.

Somehow I know this new lover even though I hadn't actually met her yet. The review plays out as I watch on totally absorbed - we find a really cool flat together, which is situated about ten miles outside of Aberdeen. There's a feeling of relief and I understand that I'm escaping this unnamed girl's tiny room, which I can only assume is some sort of students' residence that we had been cohabiting in somewhere in the centre of Aberdeen city. Then I see myself on an old racing bike cycling out of Aberdeen in the pissing rain, which is strange because I have never been to Aberdeen nor its surrounding area, yet, I know and recognise the place like the back of my hand. Also, I don't own a racing bike; but I somehow recognise the bike, *this is my bike!*

As I watch on, I witness myself pedalling slowly through what looks like the regal gates of a slightly run down manor house. Geoffrey seems very impressed that I had actually cycled in the pouring rain all the way from Aberdeen just to have a gander at his flat. He seems surprisingly okay with the fact that this future me seems to be jobless, and would as a result be claiming housing benefit in order to pay the rent.

Hold on a moment, *what happened to the skateboard ramp I was running back in Thurso?* This review of my future was getting rather confusing; I was struggling to keep up. I heard the voice of Alan again. "Danny, I must go now, I don't have time to show you anymore, but it was nice to meet you, goodbye for now." Alan's kind-hearted voice slowly faded away. *Where the bloody hell does he think he's going? I mean, how can you just appear as a strange voice in someone's head, show them some random part of their future, say a few inexplicable things that are near impossible to understand, and then, simply fuck off? What's that all about? And anyway, who the fuck is Alan Watts? I've never heard of him.*

Like a dream without any reason or meaning there is a sensation of drifting further upwards until I find myself looking down at a bus stop on a quiet back street of semi-detached Victorian red brick houses in a place that feels a lot like Glasgow. Although, I could be wrong, but it just had that feeling of being somewhere in Glasgow. A young fair-haired guy is stood at the bus stop glancing over nervously at the disturbing spectacle of a drunk nut-job staggering about dressed in a candy pink bunny onesie.

Erratically, the scary bunny-man starts punching the hell out of an old decaying brick wall a few yards from where the bus stop is situated. THUD, THUD, THUD; the dull skelps keep a sluggish beat as the blood starts oozing from his hands, slowly discolouring the candy pink coloured sleeves of the bunny suit. The young lad looks pretty scared as he watches the horrific self-harming going on before him. I want to help, but like all nightmarish dreams, I am just the observer.

The lad graciously tries to ignore it, until he can't bear it any longer. Cautiously, he skulks nearer and nearer, but at the same time keeping just enough of a safe distance between him and the crazed man. He tries to negotiate with the man to stop injuring himself. "Hey, hey, what's going on? You're doing yourself some real damage there mate."

THUD, THUD, THUD, the crazy man carries on punching the wall, harder and harder. Then the lad raises his voice unintentionally, "don't do THAT!" The crazy man stops for a moment, and then smacks the wall as hard as he can with his forehead. The lad looks away for a moment, sickened by the ferocity of it all. Gradually, the crazy man turns towards the lad with blood running down his face, oddly, he appears to have his eyes closed as if he were blind? He snaps at the lad with a strange demonic vigour. "Fuck off and don't gies any of yir patter! I'm knocking this wall doon, do ye get me laddie, do ye get me? I'M KNOCKING IT DOON! AYE, KNOCKING IT DOON - HEH, HEH, HEH. I'M KNOCKING IT DOON, DO YE HEAR ME LADDIE? HEH, HEH, HEH. I'M KNOCKING IT DOON - HEH, HEH, HEH. DO YE GET ME?"

THUD, THUD, THUD - the drunkard keeps pummelling into the wall. The lad watches on for a moment not knowing what else to do, and then he wanders off back to the bus stop, still shaking his head in total disbelief. The bus shows up. The lad gets on the bus and carries on watching the gruesome scene for a few more moments. The bus slowly pulls away. THUD, THUD, THUD - then, the thudding sound changes, and to my absolute amazement the wall starts to collapse. The crazy man starts pulling and ripping at it with his blood-gunged hands until he reveals a silver platter with a large dome-shaped lid on it. It appears to be floating on a cloud of dark smoke. The derelict remainder of an old Victorian building stands in the background.

The crazy man falls to his knees and starts to weep uncontrollably. The silver platter floats nearer to the man, who is still kneeling down in the blood-gunged bunny suit. He raises his head up and then reaches out, cautiously lifting the lid to uncover a decapitated rabbit's head, *the very same rabbit's head I'd seen near my house - the pet rabbit!* My mind races for answers as the platter hovers in mid-air for a few moments, and then, to my absolute horror it starts coming towards me while puffing out more and more smoke. Bizarrely, I'm struck with the awful pong of stale tobacco.

The silver platter hovers in front of me as the rabbit's eyelids open, revealing only empty sockets. Tears of blood trickle down its sad furry face and then without any warning, it sprays this rancid yellow spit at me whilst letting out an awful shrieking scream. The crazy man in the bunny suit starts to cackle at me with a devilish fervour from below. I'm overwhelmed by a veil of dark fog that smothers me with more of the musty tobacco smell.

WABBITS

I'm standing in a field of long grass, straight away I recognise this field, even the stench of the poisoned air coming from the sinister-looking steel works that blights the horizon is instantly familiar. I know this place well, this is the wasteland at the back of the street where I was brought up for the first seven years of my life; this is the field at the back of Stephenson Way, Corby! I watch on as if caught in a waking dream as my dear old Uncle Hamish stands perfectly still like a statue, ready to pounce, instantly reminding me of Norman Wisdom, I laugh.

Then without any warning Uncle Hamish rugby dives onto what he thinks is a rabbit hiding in the long grass. There are a few moments of struggle, then a massive owl flaps off and upward making a menacing squawking sound. My uncle's whippet, Prince, chases after the owl while snarling with the pure exhilaration of it all.

Shielding my eyes I watch the owl rise higher and higher in the sky as the sun silhouettes its magnificent form. My uncle comes over to me seething, cursing and swearing at himself; I quickly twig that he must have leaped onto a nest; he's covered in gloopy egg yolk and bits of broken eggshell. He's pretty upset about the whole matter as he calls Prince away from the nest; the dog comes over all meek, while wagging its tail, and then it drops the body of a featherless baby owl at my uncle's feet. Hamish gives the dog a nod of approval; the dog eats the baby owl. A gruesome sight, I feel appalled as the dog tears at the tiny carcass. Looking up into the bright sunlit sky again I see the owl circling from above, still squawking, and then it dawns on me that this is not squawking, but weeping. The sense of loss is powerful and I'm filled with overwhelming sensations of déjà vu. I feel sad.

"I'm sorry, Danny, I thought it was a bleddy rabbit, I didn't mean to squash the owl's eggs like that."

My uncle looks glum as he takes his filthy tartan shirt off and ties it around his waist and then he picks me up and puts me on his shoulders while calling to his dog with a high pitched whistle. So strange for me to hear that familiar whistle again. There are tears falling down his face. The first time I had ever seen him cry like that ... it's really strange to feel his presence around me again. The dream within a dream slowly fades.

I loved my uncle Hamish and I always treasured those memories of wandering around that bit of wasteland with him where we lived in Corby back in the 1970s. Uncle Hamish was always very kind to my brother, and me, especially when we were kids. He was married to my mum's sister - May. They were unable to have children because of my auntie having her womb taken out when she was young, so my brother and I were kind of like their adopted kids, in a way. Uncle Hamish loved children, all the kids that lived on Stephenson Way also loved our uncle, he would play footy out in the street with some of the older lads, he was a very popular man, and very much loved by everybody who knew him. His thing was making people laugh; he was always playing the comedian.

He worked at the Weetabix factory, doing nightshifts mainly. After he had taken his daytime kip it was his normal routine to take his dogs for a wander, and occasionally he would take his ferrets and nets with him to do a bit of poaching. I guess we were too young to really understand that what he was doing was illegal, but my brother and I loved these mini adventures out and about with Hamish.

Sometimes he would come back with anything up to ten rabbits at a time, where we would watch on totally captivated as he skilfully gutted and skinned the bunnies one after the other as he sat on his usual spot; the back door step. Once he was done he would line them all up on the lawn, pick out the best ones to store as meat and give the rest to his dogs; a wee reward for being such proficient hunters.

Sadly my uncle's hobby as a virtuoso exterminator of rabbits came to an abrupt ending for a period of time when he was caught and arrested by the police near the steel works' railway line; he was done for trespassing on private property, for poaching on private property and damaging private property. Apparently, when they snuck up on him, the poor bugger had his head jammed in the opening of a massive rabbit warren, as he tried to rescue one of his ferrets that had become stuck within the dark labyrinth.

The ferret nearly bit one of the copper's fingers clean off after an hour-long mission to successfully rescue it, this was not done out of kindness to save the poor creature, I may add, but because it was considered an essential piece of evidence to conclude the charge of poaching. Apparently, Hamish stood there in handcuffs laughing his head off while watching the coppers freaking out trying to prise the riled ferret off of their colleague's finger. Of course, this didn't really help my uncle's circumstances much when they eventually got him back to the police station.

I'll never forget the look on Aunty May's face when two policemen showed up at her door with Prince the whippet, and a cloth sack with two ferrets wriggling inside and another sack that held thirteen dead bunnies. By sheer coincidence my brother and I were playing football in her back garden at the time because Mum was at work and Dad was catching some sleep on nightshifts. We watched on as the two policemen explained the situation to our auntie, who was clearly distraught. One of the policemen told her that they no longer needed the dog, ferrets and sack of dead rabbits as evidence anymore, seeing as Uncle Hamish had admitted to the crime. She reluctantly took the cloth sacks and politely thanked the two policemen as they left.

Once they were gone Aunty May stood at the backdoor for a moment, speechless, with both sacks held tightly in her left hand. Finally, she snapped out of it, shook her head and went through to the garden to put the ferrets back in their hutch, which was always a tricky business because they were normally only ever handled by Hamish.

As soon as she was done with that she reached into the sack of dead bunnies and started placing them onto the ground to see if they were still fresh enough to use as dog meat. However, when she reached deep into the sack for the last one she realised it was half alive with a massive chunk of its face bitten off. With tears running down her cheeks she handed the bunny to my brother to put the poor thing out of its misery. Karl point blank refused. She handed it to me. So, I gripped its ears with one hand and then gave a quick tug on its back legs with my other hand until the neck gave a little click, just as my uncle had taught me. The bunny gave a pathetic squeal. The deed was done.

Aunty May took us over the road to our house to get Dad out of his bed to break the bad news to him, also, she needed a lift in his car to the police station to bail Hamish out of the clink; Dad wasn't very amused, I can tell you. Luckily for Hamish he was only given a caution and a small fine; however, to his shame, the crime was reported in the local newspaper.

Shortly after this Mum and Dad moved us up to Thurso, which kind of had a knock-on effect that finally swayed my aunty, who was being pestered by Uncle Hamish to move back up to dear old Scotland. Although, instead of making the move to Thurso where we were based, my uncle decided that he and Aunty May would move to Orkney, probably because Aunty May didn't like her husband's family too much. Keeping in mind our mum and her sister were Irish, also, Aunty May was a devoted Catholic and went to church most days.

Our dad and Uncle Hamish's lot consisted of their dear old mother, three sisters and a brother who were all born and raised in Thurso and had never left the town, unlike my dad and uncle. My dad's mother was totally bigoted towards the Irish, especially Irish Catholics. This hatred of the Irish was intensified by the actions of the IRA who were waging terrorist warfare on the British people at the time.

My dad and his brother were very close, but they were also very different people from each other, my uncle had a great sense of humour and was always good fun to be around; Dad on the other hand, was moody and cynical, very much the dour Scotsman. The frequent visits and sleepovers as small children sort of came to an abrupt end when we all moved up to Scotland, mostly because our aunty and uncle were living over the water in Orkney. Once I was old enough to travel the ferry on my own from Scrabster harbour I would occasionally go over for short breaks and holidays. It was always nice to see my uncle waiting for me as I got off the ferry. I loved staying at their house, which was situated on farmland that they rented off of a local farmer with whom they had become good friends.

My brother Karl by this time had become a teenager, so he wasn't too fussed about spending time with his uncle and aunty anymore. Anyway, he couldn't handle the choppy sea journey due to suffering from acute seasickness; it was unbelievable how unwell he would get on the ferry, even on a calm day. Luckily for me I didn't suffer from seasickness, even on a rough day the ferry ride never bothered me.

This was my first real taste of independence as a young lad and I loved it, mainly because my uncle always made me giggle and gave me a bit of attention. It was nice to be allowed to stay up late and watch movies with him. Hamish loved horror movies the best; it was great fun spooking ourselves out with all those old black and white Frankenstein and Dracula movies that we would watch over and over again while chomping on crisps and chocolate. These were really happy times for me; I loved my uncle.

Dad never seemed to enjoy being around kids, least of all his own two boys. It's not that he was purposefully horrible to us, he could be okay at times, kind-hearted even, but generally, he just ignored us, not in a bad way, I may add. No, just in that he never paid much heed to us, except when we were being unruly, then he'd come down on us with an iron fist of authority. Not someone you really want to piss off or mess with on a bad day - as I say, he had a vicious temper that often unleashed a violence of unprompted ferocity. You could tell he was not a happy man, a man full of pent-up anger - a man full of regrets! Nevertheless, unbeknownst to my brother and me his heart would soften as the years drifted by, but that's a different story.

Aye, it was a joy for me to be over in Orkney spending time with my aunty and uncle, they seemed to be upbeat about everything, and clearly enjoyed their lives, and were always happy to have me around. As luck would have it, their house was situated near to the Standing Stones of Stenness, which was within walking distance of a bigger stone circle - The Ring of Brodgar, originally consisting of sixty stones, of which only twenty-seven remain standing.

Of course, at the time I had no idea what these upright stone circles dating from the late Neolithic period with their ditches and causeways actually meant, nor did my uncle, even though he would never admit it. He always fobbed me off with some story of each stone representing a fallen Pictish king from a time before the land was even known as Scotland. Needless to say, I could tell he was making it all up, but I didn't mind his pretend history lessons, they always caught the moment, somehow stirring up the fabled magic of the place.

I was a lad when I spent my time wandering around those incredible monuments, and all I knew at the time was that they were very, very old, which somehow made them powerful - especially when they caught the evening sunlight after a hot day. Thinking about it, they were even more impressive in the winter when the snow was thick on the ground, which would make all the surrounding Neolithic monuments stand out from the white landscape.

Orkney had worked out pretty good for my uncle. He was well chuffed when he got offered his dream job working for the farmer who had also become his landlord and friend. Hamish's duties consisted of looking after the horses, helping with the general upkeep of the farm and dealing with the cattle from time to time. But the cherry on the cake for him was that his main responsibility was taking care of exterminating as many rabbits as possible, seeing as they were in such colossal numbers and causing serious damage to the crops. This was perfect for Uncle Hamish; he hated rabbits, and saw them as nothing but vermin.

He upped his game and bought a shotgun after making a pact with a local butcher shop to provide them with fresh rabbit meat to supply the hotels and restaurants in Kirkwall. My uncle was back in business!

Hamish was cleaning his new gun as me and my dad sat at his kitchen table one day, Dad asked him why he needed such a powerful gun to shoot rabbits with. He looked at my dad for a moment with a perplexed expression on his face before responding, "Rabbits? I'm not just shooting bleddy rabbits!"

Dad pondered for a second, then asked the question, "So, what else are you shooting?"

Uncle Hamish was quick to give an answer, "I'm shooting anything that fucking-well moves!" Then he gave Dad a piercing look, quickly followed by that signature death-rattle laugh of his. He got up from his chair carefully putting the gun back in its soft leather bag, then hung it off a hook on the back of the door and casually started picking dead rabbits out of a black bin liner. Hamish proceeded to skin the rabbits on bits of old newspaper that he'd placed on the kitchen floor.

In silence me and my dad watched on as Hamish held the rabbit by the back legs while gathering a bunch of skin around the ankles, twisting the skin until it snapped. Then, with a gentle yank of the fur on both rear legs he peeled back the skin until it reached the head, this made a gentle ripping sound. Pulling out his locking hunting knife from his trouser pocket he skilfully cut off both feet, then carefully proceeded to cut down the belly through the rib cage and pelvis, and then he gently scooped out the windpipe, guts and heart in one fast movement with three fingers, quickly flicking it in a plastic carrier bag.

One after another he chopped their heads off with one brisk slice of the razor sharp knife, then callously, he chucked the now full carrier bag of rabbit parts in the bin. Uncle Hamish looked over at me and my dad with a cruel smirk on his face as he continued to wash the headless skinned rabbit bodies under the running tap for a few moments in order to get rid of the surplus blood and fleshy bits. He signalled to Dad with a nod to open the lid of the massive box freezer, which was situated by the back door. My old man quickly stubbed his fag out in the ashtray and then stepped over to the box freezer, lifting the door open as my uncle started slinging in the pitiful little bodies. His butchery skills were exceptional.

The older I got the more I realised that my uncle had a bit of a thing about killing little creatures. One time when I showed up at his door unannounced after making the decision to take my bike over with me on the ferry, I found him in the garden sat on his knees with his back turned to me. "I'm over here, Danny," he muttered in an unsettled voice. As I pushed my bike up to the far end of the garden I couldn't help wondering what the hell he was up to, then I stopped in my tracks, completely horrified to witness him drowning kittens in a bucket full of water.

"Why are you doing that?" I asked, mortified.

He casually responded, "Ach, these bleddy cats are breeding like rabbits, I canny afford to feed so many bleddy cats, sure, we've already got twenty-three of the lazy whelps, and they're supposed to be keeping the rats away from the hoose - aye, my arse they are! I keep spotting rats in the barn where the horses are kept, sure, I had to stove one of the wee feckers in the heid with my shovel only just this morning; in case it bit one of the dogs, little bastards will go for anything if they're cornered, mind!" I watched on, speechless, as he chatted away oblivious to the pathetic struggle of the little kittens in his coarse hands as he cold-bloodedly plunged them into the bucket of icy cold water until the life seeped from them.

Once he had completed the evil deed he put the sodden bodies into a plastic bag then proceeded to dig a shallow grave near the compost heap. Remorselessly, he slung the plastic bag into the hole and quickly covered the bag over with a few shovels of soil, while chuffing away on a tobacco roll up that was skilfully balanced between his upper and lower lips throughout the whole operation.

There was another occasion, some years later when he was giving me a lift to the ferry, by a quirk of fate we spotted a large male rabbit on the road bathing in the sunshine, and of course my crazy uncle hit the accelerator pedal as hard as he could. Briefly, his face morphed into that of a deranged dog, I looked on aghast as the vehicle gradually caught up with the bunny that was now running as fast as its little legs could possibly go. The poor thing ran directly onto the left hand dirt track of the road. A fatal decision! Hamish jolted the steering wheel, nearly toppling the car into a ditch trying to line up the front wheels to crush the little furry creature. Closer and closer, I could see the white fluffy tale bobbing up and down like crazy, until it vanished from my sight. Before I could act in response I felt a judder to my side of the car, somehow I knew ... Uncle's work was done.

I envisioned its paltry bunny soul floating upward to pastures green to the theme tune of *Watership Down - Bright Eyes* sung just how Singing Simon had sung it back at school. My poetic muse was quickly interrupted as my uncle slammed down on the brakes whilst letting out a crazed cowboy - "Yee ha!" Followed by that familiar death-rattle-laugh which only ever surfaced when he killed rabbits.

Still snorting with delight he nipped out of the car, and I watched him through the passenger mirror as he picked up the road kill, quickly stuffing it into a carrier bag, which he always seemed have on his person. He had a quick look about to see if there was any other traffic and then he ran back to the car, looking well pleased with himself. Once he was back in the driving seat he gave me a funny look then tossed the carrier bag onto my lap, I flinched at first, not knowing quite how to react.

Without another word said between us he drove me to the ferry. I could still feel the warmth of the dead bunny's limp corpse through the plastic bag. Nausea arose within me and for a moment I really felt like I was going to puke all over the dashboard, while tactfully placing the carrier bag between my legs on the floor. Uncle Hamish just looked ahead, driving like a crazed hillbilly, sniggering to himself. I was having serious misgivings about his wild behaviour, thankfully I had put my seatbelt on that day; I never felt that safe sitting in a car with the mad bugger.

Despite all of this bloodthirstiness towards certain little furry creatures, Uncle Hamish was actually alright. Being with him was kind of like hanging out with a feral Norman Wisdom, never a dull moment was had, and there was always something funny going on with him, there was always laughter. To be fair, most animals loved him and he dearly loved them back, more so than he did with humans.

He treated his dogs like little children, much to the annoyance of everyone else in the family, me included, I may add. Dad would moan like fuck at him for letting his dogs sit on the chairs and sofa. Mum saw this as unhygienic, but then again, she was known for having some sort of weird obsessive-compulsive disorder about germs and hygiene; everything appeared to be germ-infested to her. She was constantly washing her hands and bleaching the toilets in our house, and then there was the constant nagging at Dad and me, mostly for pissing on the toilet seat and splashing the floor.

She would reprimand our uncle whenever he visited our house, when he would show up unannounced with his pesky mutts, (a Jack Russell, an Irish wolfhound and his old favourite - Prince) who would gang up and fight with our pet dog on sight. This often turned into a panicked rabble trying to pull them apart and lock them in separate rooms before they actually killed each other. Uncle Hamish found the whole thing hilarious, his familiar death-rattle echoed around the house as Dad freaked out trying to keep the dogs apart.

As far as my uncle was concerned, his dogs were his children, so where he went, the dogs went; too bad if they fought with other dogs. Aunty May mostly tolerated her husband's love for his dogs, but the truth was, she was also a bit guilty of seeing these fully-grown mutts as her little children too.

As I say, this was something that really irritated my parents; they hated the idea of a pet being treated as a child, a dog was just a dog in their eyes. Our dog, a border collie called Shep, was mostly stuck in the house, getting one meal and two short walks a day by either my brother or me. We always fought over whose turn it was, and whomever our dad nominated would have to take on the task, regardless of weather.

This was a chore that was always done reluctantly and under protest. Shep was a bit neurotic and had poor eyesight, but he was mostly a faithful old dog; the only bad thing about Shep was his urge to get into full-on fights with other dogs. The moment he saw another dog he went in for the kill, no barking or growling involved, just kill. This was highly embarrassing; it was always a risk letting him off his lead for a piss. This was one of the reasons why we only ever took Shep out for his walk late at night or early in the morning; there was less chance of banging into other people.

Our dad was pretty strict on the dog, but then, thinking about it, he was pretty strict with my brother and me too; this would sometimes instigate arguments with Aunty May. As I say, she loved children, animals, and God - this combined with the fact that she was married to Dad's brother, didn't sit too well with him.

He didn't like these qualities in a woman; he hated any form of religion and couldn't get his head around the idea of his brother being marched off to Mass every Sunday, and by a woman! But the thing that really bugged Dad about his sister-in-law was her kindness towards my brother and me. He saw this as her little way to get at him, challenging his authority. Likewise, Aunty May wasn't too keen on our dad; this was kind of understandable seeing as he always seemed to be mean-hearted and uncharacteristically quiet whenever he was in her company.

Personally, I loved my aunty May very much and I spent a fair bit of my youth sitting in her kitchen eating her delicious homemade soda bread or her yummy scones and drinking endless cups of strong tea. Most of all, I loved all the funny stories about Uncle Hamish. One story I remember her telling me about was when our dad and Hamish both got jobs working as porters in Kettering General Hospital, which involved moving unclaimed bodies from the wards to the mortuary.

On the first morning of the new job they were given instructions to collect the body of an old man from the geriatrics ward who had sadly passed away the night before. The hospital's mortuary was in the basement, which meant they had to wheel the dead body into the porter's lift, which, by sheer bad luck, broke down, with them inside, trapping them in-between floors. After an hour or so, the smell coming off of the corpse was becoming pretty unbearable. They were starting to wonder if anyone had actually noticed that the lift was out of action, seeing as it was a lift that was only ever used specifically to move corpses down to the mortuary.

Then it suddenly dawned on them both that they were the only two porters on that particular job that morning, which meant there was a reasonable chance that no one had even noticed the lift. A few hours passed by, and then without any warning, and to their absolute horror, the dead man's body started letting out gases with a massive burping sound. This of course, made the body jerk upright on the trolley with only the whites of his eyes staring straight at the two brothers. Dad and Hamish totally freaked out, thinking the old man had come back from the dead.

Apparently they screamed like lunatics, then, as if by magic, the lift started moving downwards. As soon as the doors opened they both made their escape, running off in different directions, leaving the body hanging awkwardly off of the trolley, held only by a thin strap that went across the waist. They never went back, both of them were deeply disturbed by the whole drama. Even though they laugh about it now, it was no joke at the time; they were truly spooked.

Sadly as I got older I saw less and less of my uncle and aunt, especially when I became ill with leukaemia. I must admit to being a bit shocked when I went over to visit them shortly after I was given the all clears, it'd been nearly two years since I had seen either of them. When I say shocked, what I really mean is, I was saddened to witness my poor old aunt, now in her late seventies, suffering from acute osteoporosis. She had become all hunched and couldn't use her neck properly, and it was clear she was in a lot of pain. Fair play to her though, she still put on a brave face and kept conversation light.

Poor old girl was reaching the end of her years, which was sad for my uncle because he was fifteen years younger than his wife. Uncle Hamish had his own health problems going on, a collapsed lung and angina, mostly caused by a poor diet and smoking too much. I really got a sense of the passing of time, seeing them fading with old age.

Unbeknownst to me, that particular visit would turn out to be the last time I would wander with Hamish and the dogs, who were also getting on a bit. Prince, his favoured and much loved whippet, was not as fast as he used to be and was straining to catch a rabbit these days, the other two dogs were worse.

After wandering the fields for a short while my uncle's eyes lit up as he and the dog stopped in their tracks. I tried to work out what they were all looking at, and then I spotted it. At the far end of the field sat a jet-black rabbit, of course, my uncle's only thought was to kill it. The dogs took off at speed. At first the rabbit was oblivious to the dogs, then it heard them charging towards it, the rabbit ran right around the field, but Prince started catching up. Then I noticed the rabbit turning as the other two dogs caught it out from the opposite direction, snapping at its ankles like lions going in for the kill. It turned again and again, trying to shake the dogs off.

Then a weird thing happened, the rabbit started running straight towards me, I didn't really know what to do, I had no time to think, I couldn't bear the thought of the dogs ripping this poor bunny apart. *Anyway surely it must be someone's pet rabbit, because you don't get black rabbits living in the wild*, I thought as the rabbit ran straight past me, I could see Prince wasn't far behind. It was at that split second that I made the decision to get in the whippet's way.

The mutt smashed into my legs and knocked me clean off my feet, yelping and howling as it rolled into a heap. Prince had a cut leg and was limping and whining in pain as I rolled about, feeling like I had been kicked in the shins by a psychotic schoolgirl. Uncle Hamish stood there staring at me; he was absolutely livid. He wanted to kill that bunny and I prevented that from happening as well as injuring his precious Prince. "Right, you, get in that car!" he hollered at me, while pointing to his car, which was parked about half a mile away at the far end of the field. And that was that! The last time I ever went for a walk with my uncle. Sadly my aunty May died some months later, and was older than I thought; she was actually eighty-two.

Hamish was never the same after the death of his wife. It has always bothered me that we ended our lifetime adventures together on bad terms. I saw him a few times after that, when he came over the water to see his brothers and sisters, but it was clear that he was not the same man that I knew as a child. He looked so sad and lost without his wife, old age and ill health slowly but surely dimming that humorous spark within him. It was like someone had turned the lights off from behind his eyes.

In spite of this, there was one weird disjointed conversation I remember having with him in the front room of our house. I'm not too sure what instigated the discussion but I think it was because I asked him how many rabbits he reckoned he must have exterminated in his life. He grinned at me. "Do you know, Danny, I must have killed thousands and thousands of rabbits. My dear mother, God rest her soul, told me once, that if you ever witness a rabbit spitting then that's a sign that it's casting a curse on you!"

I looked at him with a sarcastic smirk on my face and asked him, "Have you ever seen a rabbit spit?"

He smiled back at me as his eyes welled up with tears, "Aye, I've been cursed alright." That was the last time I ever saw him.

The years drifted by and I got on with my life trying to recover from my battle with cancer, Uncle Hamish became very reclusive and didn't come over the water to Thurso anymore. Apparently, the day before he died he went out wandering the streets in a peculiar, but happy mood, and gave everything he owned away to complete random strangers, including his old dogs. Our dad caught word of his odd behaviour from some of his neighbours who phoned our house, concerned that the old boy had lost the plot.

Sadly, by the time Dad got over on the ferry the next day, he discovered his brother lying face down in the fields behind his house, right next to a massive rabbit warren, still in his pyjamas and nightgown. Uncle Hamish had suffered a heart attack. Dad took the death of his brother really badly; it changed him forever.

Spit the Blood - Cast the Spell!

Spit the blood; cast the spell, and blight their dreams, again and again with burning blisters, splintering wheezes, runny noses and exploding sneezes! Spit the blood; cast the spell, curses on those humans who stretched the necks of the furry ones that fell. Spit the blood; cast the spell, and blight their dreams, over and over with constant yearning, biting breezes, fidgety scratching, frozen and freezing from frostbitten squeezing!

Spit the blood; cast the spell, curses on those who chopped off the paws and peeled back the skin of the furry ones that fell. Spit the blood; cast the spell, curses on those humans, and curses on their evil hounds, as well! Spit the blood; cast the spell, let us haunt their tiny minds, and poison their ghastly ferrets with an unbearable smell! Spit the blood; cast the spell, curses on those evil assassins, blight them all with endless nightmares, blight them all with unending hell!

Daffy Duck Kicked Your Arse!

One eye slowly opened as the smell of shit hit the back of my parched throat, more waves of nausea ran through me, I sensed the burden of being back in my body again. It felt dense. My sweaty face peeled off of the cubicle wall like sellotape, leaving a smudge that looked nothing like me imprinted on the plastic coated wall.

I was still crouched on the toilet seat with my jeans at my ankles. *At least the shit has stopped squirting out of my arse;* I reassured myself, feeling astonished to be back from the dead. *I'm alive? Maybe it was just a whitey and not a near death experience, after all?* This was not a good time to be brooding over such matters, so I went about cleaning myself off, which resulted in me accidently blocking the toilet up with shit and bog roll. No matter how many times I flushed the toilet, it was no good; it was properly blocked.

Ah, fuck it! I told myself, while pulling my jeans up and subconsciously tightening my belt buckle. That's when I noticed how much my hands were shaking. I started fiddling with the lock of the cubicle door, which quickly turned into an agitated struggle, but finally, I managed to pull the damn thing open; it clattered, making me flinch. My legs had gone, but somehow I glided over to the nearest sink.

Immediately, I sensed a Grey reptilian gadgie to my left taking a piss in one of the urinals; pretending not to care, I washed my hands and then splashed some water over my face. Feeling seriously dehydrated; I took a long drink from the tap, but took little pleasure from it. *"What is it with this crunching bollocks?"* I hissed at myself, the Grey gave me a suspicious look as I heard the unmistakable sloshing sound of piss hitting the aluminium urinal with force; he let out a snake-like sigh of relief.

Without warning he stomped over to the sink next to me, washed his long webbed hands, took a look in the mirror to straighten his plastic bunny ears that were stretched across his big egg-shaped head. He caught me staring at him and then muttered, "All right, pal?"

"Aye, nae bother. What's with the bunny ears everyone's wearing tonight?" My response was polite, but to the point. He looked at me with his black almond eyes for a brief moment, like I'm the stupid one.

"Och, it's one ay promotional freebees tae dae wi the new Peggy Pope album, *Falling doon the bunny hole,* uir boss said it was one ay weird requirements Peggy insisted on before accepting the gig, radge is taking the pure pish, but whit can ye dae, eh?"

Rolling my eyes politely I gave a friendly smile back at him in the mirror, realising he was one of the other bar staff. Then, like a balloon caught in a summer breeze I drifted over to the electric dryer to dry my hands before making my escape out the door. Though, I couldn't stop worrying about the blocked toilet and the rancid stench that was wafting out of the cubicle, *fuck; what if they suss it was me that blocked their toilet?* Feeling pretty troubled about the situation I was suddenly side-tracked by the wary glare of the reptilian barman as he stood behind the bar pretending to clean a pint glass with a towel. I drifted by, avoiding any eye contact with the sly fecker.

The place had filled up with more Greys, all dressed like humans, and all of them wearing the same daft-looking bunny ears. *What the fuck is that all about, how come I never heard or read anything about this new Peggy album?* I asked myself. There were quite a few humans filling the place up too, mostly local lads with their girlfriends who were doubtless unaware of who Peggy Pope was, and most likely hearing word around town that he'd been on Top of the Pops a few times back in the early 1980s. *They'll be in for a shock tonight!* I thought as a smug grin stretched across my face on spotting my pals.

"And where the fuck have you been for the last hour?" snapped Fergus, who was looking really worried.

"I was taking a shit in the bogs," I answered. Cormag handed a fresh pint to me. The lights were turned low as that familiar *wha-wha* drone mixed with a *ping-pong* looped beat that slowly built and built, eventually reaching full pelt; this could only be the music of the mythical - Peggy Pope! A mixture of locals and lizard folk made their way to the foot of the stage, while others sat in groups around candlelit tables. We had a fantastic view of the stage and a table full of beers in front of us. *Thank fuck that whitey phase is over!* I thought, relieved to have not missed the gig.

My mood lightened as waves of euphoria welled up inside, turning into bubbles of pure warmth that connected me to everyone in the room, including our lizard friends - the Greys! Everything seemed to sparkle like glitter, bliss radiated from everything, I mean, what can I say - I was feeling bloody marvellous! For the first time in my life it felt like

I was free from my wretched existence, this was the real me and I was blissed out of my fucking skull!

Peggy Pope stepped out of the shadows and onto the stage wearing large retro sunglasses, tight leopard print leggings with a pair of Daffy Duck boxer shorts pulled over them, and a leopard print shirt; his long golden hair was bunched up like a drunken schoolgirl's. He looked like a cross between Iggy Pop and a lanky Neolithic 'Pebbles' from '*The Flintstones*,' cartoon, either way he clearly didn't give a rat's ass what anyone thought of him, he was totally fearless! Lizards and locals gathered in larger numbers at the front of the stage to get a closer look at the aging rock star.

Before Peggy even got a chance to speak into the microphone, a crowd of townie twats dressed in denim jackets and lumberjack shirts started chanting the word, "buffty, buffty, buffty . . ." from some tables situated right at the back of the room. To my sheer delight Peggy took off his guitar, and then stepped over from the side of the stage directly onto our table, we all grabbed at our pint glasses for fear of spillage. Peggy just gave us all a cracked grin and then he stepped across to the next table along, and then to the next, moving like a ballet dancer on his tippy toes until he got to the table where the mob of dickheads were sitting.

He loomed over them for a moment as he fidgeted with the elastic on his Daffy Duck boxer shorts; finally he dug out a couple twenty-pound notes, which he tossed at them. He gave them all the evils from behind his dark glasses and then proceeded to step back over the pathway of tables until he eventually got back to the stage, declaring over the room via the microphone, "There's your money back, you bunch of pricks; now fuck off back to your TV sets, just like King Plank did back in the Stone Age!" At which point some heftier-looking lizard types appeared, only these ones were more human-like, but all wearing the same plastic bunny ears on their oval heads.

We all watched on as they quickly jumped in and removed the dickheads. A scuffle broke out and some chairs and tables were knocked over, but there was no contest, considering the lizard dudes were about nine feet tall and both built like brick shit houses. The dickheads were dragged out in headlocks; the crowd cheered a cry of triumph at Peggy's cool-headed pluckiness with the difficult situation. It was hilarious to think that a tall thin Englishman wearing leopard print leggings with a pair of Daffy Duck boxer shorts pulled over them and with his hair bunched up like a girl, could make a gang of knuckle-dragging farmer boys from the hills look like a bunch of Muppets. *Heh; classic!*

Peggy stared out at the crowded room through his big retro sunglasses, and then signalled to the guy at the mixing desk to take the backing music down a bit so everyone could hear the comical clatters of the fight going on between the lizard bouncers and the dickheads just outside the main entrance. The place went quiet for a moment as everyone listened to the sounds of flesh being punched and bones being broken, which echoed through the half opened doors.

There was a call across the room to the bar staff from one of the lizard bouncers who had stuck his head around the door, to phone for the police, and an ambulance. Everyone in the room looked up at Peggy as he indicated to the sound guy to turn the volume up again. A big trippy grin lit up his face while he calmly notified us all in his posh accent, but with a true sense of the moment: that his Daffy Duck shorts were impregnated with LSD! The crowd gave a loud cheer of approval! Then he went on to tell everyone about his new album: *Falling Down the Bunny Hole!*

So, he has got a new album coming out then! Without any further ado, he broke into a nine-minute vocal mantra that echoed around the room like a chanting Tibetan monk; no one gave him any grief from that point onwards! The music ensued and it was mind-altering, it was loose, but tight and with a coherent meaning that confused the hell out of me, yet delighted me in equal measure.

This was a real happening of the highest order and every moment was a joy to my ears, not just because I was off my tits, but more because this English poet was like some kind of high priest bringing us all into direct contact with something so wonderfully perfect and *far out!* This was a psychedelic mother ship smashing through the glass roof of reality! Everything about this tall Englishman was psychedelic, yet so fucking righteous, this man rocked with the stage presence of Iggy Pop, but with the weird splendour of Merlin.

The kiddies weren't too sure how to take the first few moments, but it wasn't long before they were all jumping up and down at the front of the stage like bouncing babies. All I could do was watch on from our table, my legs were still gone; moving wasn't an option anymore. None of this mattered, I was just glad that we had actually made it here, against all the bizarre odds that stacked up against us, what with Fergus predicting that the Banana Splits could show up at my door uninvited, and me temporarily turning into a big pussy cat only to find out I was really a weird looking sabre-toothed bunny man. Then being slimed by a giant slug, as well as finding out that Chong was actually telepathic after all! And what about all these alien cunts with the plastic bunny ears?

Yep, it had been a right mission to get here, but it was well worth the effort, yet it seemed odd knowing that Jerry and I were probably the only two feckers in the joint who actually *knew* most of the songs that were being blasted at us with precision from the old master. Peggy rocked!

Regardless of the room being full of neds, ravers, metalheads, country boys and reptilian Greys who were most probably from some fucked up parallel universe, Peggy didn't give a shit; he had the place pulsating with his sonic attack, quirky snippets of Neolithic history and cheeky banter about the fighting spirit of the Scots.

Feeling like I was caught up in a kaleidoscopic storm of unadulterated space rock, just as my mind had finally popped its sugar-coated cherry, I spotted Jerry standing at the back of the stage laughing his head off doing the pendulum thing again, but at a crazy, supersonic speed. No one really paid much attention to him at first, and for whatever reason, Peggy didn't see him either. Looking over at the big lizard men at the doors who were already revved up from dealing with the dickheads, it was pretty obvious that they were eyeing up Jerry to chuck him out too. To my absolute amazement people in the audience started swinging their arms like pendulums as well. Within seconds the whole room was swinging their arms, even the lizard bouncers were seeing the funny side of it and started swinging their arms in time to the music too.

Peggy was too caught up in his performance to even notice Jerry standing behind him, then as the song came to a psychedelic crescendo Peggy spun round, spotting him, and then started rocking his head with approval by keeping the music going on his amazing looking twelve-string guitar that sparkled when the stage lights caught it.

I couldn't help myself; I stood up and started swinging my arms in time, along with everyone in the room. It was like

Daffy Duck Kicked Your Arse!

Rock 'n' Roll Holy Communion for the dispossessed! I was getting higher and higher, and for the first time in my life I felt like I was truly sitting on cloud nine as the music pulsated every atom within me. Then, everything started going into slow motion, but in a really cool, cool way, as the room sparkled and vibrated with pure ecstasy. Everything felt so perfect. Even those alien lizard fuckers were kind of endearing in their daft bunny ear thingamabobs.

Peggy kept knocking out the tunes, one after the other with ear-splitting accuracy. I felt so much love in the room, it was like we had all come to a higher state of being and everyone understood the joy, without any need for words. This was no hippie shit, no, this was something very, very different, this, was something else and once you were there, you never wanted to come down. What a fucking buzz, watching all those arms going at it like insect wings round a honey hive - all in time and swishing at astonishing speed. Even between songs Peggy interacted with the audience like a kind of cracked, enigmatic Jesus Christ in Daffy Duck shorts, he had us all in the palm of his hand, and when he spoke you could hear a pin drop in the room, the atmosphere was electric.

On the final ovation, and believe me there were many, the bouncers finally made a lunge at Jerry who was now standing on one of the PA speakers swinging his arms in time with the audience. Luckily, Peggy spotted the bouncers and stopped them in their tracks, and then he climbed up on the opposite PA speaker and applauded Jerry. The crowd gave one last roar of gratitude; Peggy jumped off the speaker and grabbed Jerry by the arm and the two of them wandered off backstage.

Of course, we were all dribbling wrecks by this point as we all sat back down at the table, supping up the remainders of our pints. It wasn't long before the place started clearing out as we all watched on in silence as the roadies quickly dismantled the amps and put away Peggy's massive guitar collection. There was a wonderful calmness in the room; my ears were ringing from the gig as waves of pleasure vibrated through me. My heart was pumping through my chest with unadulterated satisfaction. "What now, boys?" I asked, feeling on top of the world. Everyone sitting at the table responded with a shrug of the shoulders. Then Jerry showed up, looking well chuffed with himself. "So, what have you been up to, ya bugger?" I asked in a jokey fashion.

"Oh, just having a wee spliff and a chat with your man Peggy, hey guess what?" We all looked at each other for a moment then all looked back at Jerry.

"What?" I asked. Then without saying a word he stretched his arm out with his fist clenched while signalling with a nod of the head for me to put my hand out. I put my hand out not really knowing what to expect, and he placed what at first looked like a piece of neatly folded-up coloured cardboard into the cup of my hand. Taking a closer look, along with the others, we all drew nearer to my open hand, wondering what the hell it was we were actually looking at. We stared at each other for a brief second, and then the penny dropped.

In my hand sat twenty hits of acid blotters with tiny little pictures of Daffy Duck printed on each individual segment. Jerry was pissing himself trying to contain the laughter while nodding with joy at us all as we tried hard to comprehend what the fuck was going down here. The cheeky fecker had somehow blagged twenty hits of acid, although he totally denied this, claiming that he'd been given it by one of the roadies as he left Peggy's dressing room.

We started to cackle like chimps feasting on lumps of juicy meat from a fresh kill. At lightning speed we squinted at each other mischievously and without a second thought sunk three hits of the acid each, washing it down with the last dregs of our watery pints, except Jerry, he gobbled five of the blotters in one go. We all shook our heads at the crazy fucker, knowing that this was a heroic dosage by anybody's standards! There was no looking back from here, all of us united in our lunacy; the bond felt strong and the bond felt good. We were a team.

"Shall we head back to my place then?" My suggestion was met with some eagerness as the bunny-eared reptilian barman came over to clear up the empty pint glasses from our table, I could tell the snooping fucker was trying to see what we were all up to. We sat there quietly smiling at the slithery fuckwit, not saying a word as he twitched around us. "That's it, lads, the party's over now, can ye all make yoor way oot please." We grabbed our coats; got up from our chairs and staggered out of the main doors.

The Ghost of Dowpy Duncan

The snow had finally stopped and the wind had turned into a calm breeze as the temperatures dipped even further below zero. It instantly reminded me of a scene from one of those cheesy Christmas cards from the value packs that our mum would purchase at the local charity shop. Almost immediately the acid invaded my vision and brain with that familiar anticipation, that somehow things were not exactly as they seemed.

In my mind's eye I visualised hundreds of hands and faces pushing through the fabric of reality, somehow shooting mind bullets up in the air. Mind bullets that come from the heart because the mind does not dwell in the brain or in the skull! No, the mind dwells within the heart, becoming aware of this, brought me closer to the real me, the real me who decides who I am, the entire me that isn't this fake concept of me living in this heavy meat van that I recognise as the body.

"You okay, Danny?" Jerry stood in front of me for a moment, looking like a skinny Goliath. Staring into my eyes he repeated the question, "You okay, Danny?"

"Aye, I'm fine, but this acid is coming up like a steam train, for a moment there you looked just like Goliath."

"You mean Goliath from the Bible?" he quizzed.

"Aye, Goliath from the Bible," I responded. Jerry giggled like an over-excited child for a few moments, then I noticed that the stonewall dyke behind him was glowing with rainbow colours that rippled with incandescent waves of light. *Incandescent* was a word I had never used in context in my life, nor even knew what it really meant, yet, tonight my mind realised exactly what this word meant, it seemed effortless to make sense of things that I normally wouldn't even consider. *What the fuck is happening to me?* My brain raced for answers, but there were none.

Jerry looked at me in a concerned manner, "Danny, don't fight it, mate, just roll with it, you know it's going to play with your head either way, enjoy this moment because we will all be dead before we know it."

What a strange thing to say. I smiled back at him for a moment and realised he was tripping his fucking nuts off too; his eyes were shimmering. This was a splendid feeling although I was slightly anxious about the way my thoughts were rushing through me. *What the fuck am I going on about?* I thought, trying to reason with myself, while laughing out aloud for a few moments at the absurdity of it all. Jerry started laughing, and then he stopped abruptly and pointed at the stone dyke, "Check it out, the colours ripple like a jellyfish."

"You see it too?" I asked.

"Yep!" he replied, "crazy, eh?" I nodded back at him silently as we both examined the dyke wall for a bit longer, totally spellbound by its sheer magnificence. Finally we caught up with the others, who were also pointing at the rainbow colours rippling through the dyke wall. We could see it as clear as day, which dumbfounded us all for a few more moments. There was a true sense of ill-fated delight among us as we chuckled like little children marching toward the other side of the town, making sure to take the back streets away from all the drunkards and meatheads who would be staggering about eating fish suppers and looking for a scrap outside Robyn's Fish and Chip shop.

No, none of us were in any frame of mind to be dealing with that. Thurso could be quite a dangerous place sometimes, like any small forgotten seaside town full of bored alcoholic clowns with anger issues. Aye, we all knew the score and for once no one complained about taking the longer route back to my place. In fact the walk was very pleasant, everything felt intensely beautiful, alive, familiar, yet different all at the same time. My mind wandered and wandered. Excitement heaved throughout my body, like a fizz of expectancy waiting for the black-eyed angel to show up dressed in its proverbial bulletproof suit that was crafted with fabric weaved from the fibres of human misery. *Aye, I'm on the bones of my arse and death is waiting for me at the end of the road. Yet, I feel optimistic? Why do I have so much hope?*

Thoughts were sprinting throughout every thread of my being but my revelations and insights were abruptly diverted as I scrutinised a somewhat comical spectacle that was slowly, but surely corroding my patience. Tony, Fergus and Wallace, were all having a heated discussion about how the Scottish Premier Division would end in success for Rangers over their nearest rivals Aberdeen, which would mean that they would have clinched six titles in a row. This would ultimately mean that St. Johnstone, Raith Rovers and Dundee could possibly be relegated to the first division after finishing in the bottom three positions.

Now, don't get me wrong here, normally I'm up for a wee bit of football banter, but for the life of me I couldn't understand how anyone in their right mind could focus on the imperatives of the Scottish Premier Division while tripping out like this?

"Oi, you three, shut the fuck up about footy, for the love of God, I'm gonny gouge my eyes out with invisible soup spoons if I hear another word about footy, ya bunch of fecken goons!" All three of them stopped in their tracks and looked at me as if *I* was a complete lunatic. Jerry, who was tagging behind with Cormag, and unbeknownst to me was also starting to feel riled by all this football talk, said "Yeah, Danny's right, shut the fuck up about football, it's giving me a bad trip listening to it!" Tony stepped forward and with a calm voice posed the question, "So, what do you suggest we talk about then, boys?"

Jerry barked back at him, "Well how about a bet?"

"A bet?" Wallace questioned.

"Yeah, a bet!" Jerry snapped again.

"Okay then, I bet you can't climb to the top of that lamppost!" Wallace said with a smarmy tone to his voice. Jerry looked at Wallace for a moment with that familiar impish glint in his eye, "Right, if I climb to the top of that lamppost you three must promise to not mention another word about football for the rest of the night!" All three shook Jerry's hand in turn, the deal was sealed as I struggled to understand how the hell he was going to scale up a frosty looking lamppost on a freezing night, while being off his head on psychedelics, amphetamines, ecstasy, booze and hash.

Sure as hell, Jerry scrambled up the lamppost like a chimpanzee, but true to form, freaked the bejesus out of us all when he casually swung upside down and hung like a bat by the backs of his legs. Every one of us flinched; convinced we were all about to witness a horrible accident. Jerry hung there for a moment and (weirdly) started making sheep noises. Then he let out a lurid scream that startled us all. He began to weep uncontrollably, while swinging his arms slowly, and even weirder still, his weeping transformed into hysterical laughter. Then he stopped.

"Jerry, are you okay, mate?" I asked, genuinely concerned for my dear friend. We all watched on as he wiped his eyes with the sleeves of his jumper, let out a massive sigh, then gave me that kooky smile of his.

"Think I may have tripped out a bit there - sorry, lads, sorry," he mumbled back at us.

"Jerry, are you going to come down from there, before you hurt yourself?" I suggested softly for fear of him freaking and falling head first toward the concrete curb below. He swung himself upright with the grace of an Olympic gymnast and then calmly climbed down the lamppost. We were all in total shock, speechless as the effects of the Daffy Duck blotters squeezed our brains harder and harder. We wandered off in silence like a group of spinsters going to a cat's funeral.

There was a peculiar tranquillity about everything; the icy breeze had vanished. All that could be heard was the gentle crunching sound of the frozen snow from beneath our feet. Everything was pleasing to the eye, but with a tendency to morph into something more sinister the longer you looked at it, but this time the feeling was much more intense and harder to control!

Sporadic sniggering erupted from each of us randomly, like crazed children still tippy-toeing through a disenchanted Narnia that was strewn with forgotten booby traps, purposefully placed to mystify our evolved monkey brains. It was safe to say we were all acting like a bunch of crazies on the run from the asylum, all of us recognising the symptoms, and going through the motions, all of us smirking inwardly at ourselves. The medication was relentless and brutal; everything seemed to be somehow tied in, connected and authentic.

Advancing to the other side of the footbridge over the river past the *Dammies* football grounds to the right, we could still hear the sounds of the dodgy karaoke echoing over the river from the open doorway of the British Legion as we took the usual left turn on the path toward my house. A gradual sense of fear unfurled among us as we walked into the darkness of the night, the dim glow of the last few street lamps faded behind us like a stagnant orange fog. There was silence; no one said a word. The dark silhouette of the castle ruins still looked magnificently Gothic and creepy. Cormag broke the silence as he halted abruptly.

"Hold on boys, can ye hear it, I swear I just heard a voice?"

We all stopped and listened to see if we could hear anything, but there was nothing. We carried on walking for a bit. Then, we all heard it. Sure enough, there seemed to be what sounded like a man's voice mumbling away in the darkness. Looking at each other again, there was a sudden ripple of uneasiness among us all as the muttering voice got closer, and louder. Nervously, we took a step towards each other trying to work out where the voice was coming from; it was really hard to pin down. It got louder, but seemed to be moving around us, one moment it sounded like it was coming from behind us, then the next it seemed to be coming from the opposite direction.

We clung onto each other like petrified children for a few moments, and then out of the shadows materialised a tall, hunched bearded man, dressed in a black donkey jacket with a black cap pulled tight over his head, as he stomped right past us. His face looked unnaturally pale with his eyes pointing to the ground, still muttering to himself as if he hadn't seen us. He appeared to be carrying a sack, which was slung over his right shoulder, as he chuffed away on an old-fashioned clay pipe that stuck out from his bearded mouth.

We all froze and stood to one side totally petrified, trying not to get in his way; it all happened so fast. Then a bit further on he stopped and dumped the sack on the ground, and to our total amazement a stream of wild rabbits scuttled from it, scarpering in every direction. He cursed at the rabbits while tugging away on his clay pipe as a puff of tobacco smoke wafted upwards into the frosty air and then he slung the empty sack over his shoulder and wandered off into the shadows. The air around us was suddenly engulfed with the awful musty smell of tobacco.

Instantly we all recognised who this man was, as a collective sense of relief washed over all of us; it was just a down-and-out guy called 'Dowpy Duncan' - the town's local loony. I took a second look to see if I could spot him in the shadows, but he had vanished back into the darkness just as quickly as he'd appeared.

The smell of stale tobacco lingered as we walked onwards into the dark night towards my house, it seemed near impossible to escape the dreadful pong of his clay pipe. *It was strange to bang into him like that, and what the fuck was all that business with the rabbits?* I wondered to myself, but then, everything about poor old Dowpy was a bit odd. Throughout our childhoods Dowpy was looked upon as the creepy old town tramp that our parents warned us all to steer well clear of, which we did!

Dowpy Duncan spent his life wandering the streets of Thurso passing his days away picking at the plethora of half-smoked cigarette butts outside the pubs and shops that were stuck to the pavements. He was well known for gathering

The Ghost of Dowpy Duncan

all the bits of tobacco out of the half-smoked fag butts so he could smoke it in his smelly old clay pipe.

Dowpy's real name was Duncan Black, a sinister-looking character who never really bothered anyone, yet no one messed with him either, even the hard nuts around town left Dowpy Duncan well alone. He was known for spitting in the street and would sometimes spit in the paths of people, infuriating some of the more respectable locals, while providing light entertainment for others. He was also known for being a bit erratic and bad tempered; he could be very volatile if approached by anyone he didn't like the look of, this was probably due to some form of mental illness. Holidaymakers would take photos of him, but only from a safe distance. Of course, Dowpy wasn't at all interested other than to make horrid retching noises from the back of his throat and then spit a massive blob of tobacco-tinged slobber in their paths before wandering off with his hands in his pockets while talking to himself. He always walked with his hands in his trouser pockets.

There was a rumour that his parents were very wealthy and owned two properties, a Victorian house in Thurso and a massive farmhouse not too far out of town. When they both died of old age there was a tidy sum of money left behind, all of which was inherited by Dowpy's older brother. Dowpy was given the old house in Thurso as a sort of open-handed payoff after much quarrelling with his brother over the matter, but no money ever came his way.

Dowpy became very bitter about his parents leaving him out of their will, to the point of having a complete mental breakdown, which he never recovered from. As the years rolled on the sudden news came through that Dowpy's older brother was dying, and according to the myth the last words he uttered was a threat that he would come back and haunt Dowpy if he so much as set foot inside the farmhouse, or indeed, spent any of the money that came with it.

Nevertheless, Dowpy inherited the lot as he was the last remaining member of the family. The farmhouse was never lived in from that point onwards and the place fell into a state of disrepair. Dowpy never spent any of the inheritance left to him for fear of his brother coming back from beyond the grave, the money just sat for years untouched in a post office savings account.

By this time Dowpy was totally bonkers and prone to fits of rage, whereby his neighbours could hear him smashing his place up while arguing and screaming at the supposed ghost of his long deceased brother. The old Victorian house was hidden by an overgrown garden; most of the windows had been smashed, and patched up with pieces of cardboard. Apparently, the only thing inside the house was a flea-bitten mattress that was placed in the middle of the front room, along with piles of old rubbish and plastic Irn-Bru bottles, which he burned in his fire.

As I say, apart from the police no one ever messed with Dowpy, but to be fair he generally kept himself to himself, regardless of his creepy behaviour. Often he would sleep on the benches in front of the church clock in the centre of town, snoring away without a care in the world, hands still in his trouser pockets. Other times he could be spotted down by the beach on a hot day, sipping from a slit he had made with his knife in the side of a plastic bottle of Irn-Bru; it was a mystery why he never took the lid off of a bottle and drank from it normally. I don't think anyone was ever brave enough to approach him and ask why he did this.

Our dad would occasionally catch him in the car headlights on his way back from work, where Dowpy would be sitting in the dark on the side of the road across from the lonely farmhouse, refusing to go in, preferring to sleep rough in the ditch. No one really knew why he would do this, but it was a creepy sight to behold if you were driving by on a dark night. This is all we really knew about Dowpy Duncan. He was a weird old chap who became a bit of a legend in and around Thurso.

Nothing was said as we all wandered onwards into the darkness, choosing to ignore the weird incident of stumbling into Dowpy like that, which wasn't easy considering the mind-altering headspace we were already in. The heebie-jeebies kept rattling around my fried brain as I attempted to make sense of what had just happened there. I felt a need to break the uneasy silence. "Dowpy gets about these days, eh? I don't think I've ever seen him down this way before?" Everyone just shrugged their shoulders in a sort of dumbstruck response.

The recurring urge to run as fast as possible while ripping all my clothes off came with every gust of bliss that rushed through my confused mind. Thankfully, this urge quickly passed me by, put off by all the ice and snow that stretched out on the coastal path like a frozen swamp reflecting in the moonlight. Anyway, I was trying to take Jerry's advice, and go with it, in spite of my confused state of mania. Wallace stopped in his tracks, at first I thought he was going to be sick or something; he looked overwhelmed with fear and was clearly struggling to spit out the words. Glaring at us all with a confused expression on his face before reminding us of something that we had all somehow overlooked, he said, "boys, hold on a second here, Dowpy died about six months ago!"

"Eh? No way, man!" I barked back at him, convinced he was taking the piss.

"I'm telling ye Dowpy croaked about six months ago, they found him in his hoose deid, honest to Christ, I'm telling ye the truth, it was all over the newspapers, surely ye all seen it? Half the toon came oot to his funeral."

Cormag butted in, "Jesus, boys, you know what this all means, don't you?" We all looked at him for a moment, bemused. "We've just witnessed the ghost of Dowpy Duncan! Wallace is telling the truth, Dowpy died months ago, I remember reading about it in the newspaper, right enough, aye."

"Shut up, you pair of nutters," I said, convinced they were both in on the joke trying to shit me up. *They're testing me!* I thought, I started examining their body language to see if I could spot any sneaky eye signals, but all I saw was fear mixed with bewilderment etched on their frozen coupons. Then Jerry started joining in, "Danny, they're telling the truth, mate; he died months ago, I remember seeing it in the paper too."

"Eh, then if he's deid then who was that we all just saw?" I questioned, gobsmacked. Bursting into an uneasy laughter we continued to wander on past the castle, all of us spooked out and too frightened to look back in case Dowpy would step out of the shadows again.

Tony wouldn't let it go and started quizzing the whole chain of events, "He looked so real though, and I could smell his stinky old pipe, you all smelt it, right?" We all nodded in agreement, walking faster and faster toward my house, slipping and sliding all over the place with only the moonlight to guide our way. Tony reasoned on, "Look, boys, we have to rationalise the situation here, seeing as we are all flying off our tits, aye, maybe we've had a joint hallucination or something?"

The Ghost of Dowpy Duncan

"Nah, it doesn't add up, Tony," responded Cormag in his usual calm collected manner, "Why would we all hallucinate the same thing at exactly the same moment, and why on earth would we all randomly hallucinate about Dowpy Duncan?"

Wallace jumped in, "He looked real, and as Tony pointed out, you could even smell the fecker, ken what I mean."

"Ah, but did you see how pale his face looked, it was like there was a glow coming off of it, I mean, he didn't look a normal colour; he was paler than a sheet!" I replied, slowly buying into the rather distressing notion of Dowpy's ghost. The others, except Tony, nodded in agreement with me, as each and every one of us felt like someone or something had wandered all over our collective graves.

Fergus started whimpering to himself nervously, "Fecken Nora, fecken Nora, we've all just seen the ghost of Dowpy Duncan, I can't believe it, and honest to Christ I never thought I'd ever, ever see a ghost." He looked well disturbed about the situation, while the rest of us recoiled at the very thought of what we had all just bore witness to. The Daffy Duck acid wasn't helping matters, as it did its work on all of us; there was a heavy vibe going down.

Fergus stopped and put his finger to his lips to shush us all, and then we all heard the mumbling sound again; Dowpy was near! The hair on my arms and neck stood on end as my fists clenched. Terrified, we all stood in the darkness hearing the mumbling voice move around us in every direction, and then slowly, slowly it faded off into the distance again.

Fergus started to have a proper meltdown, "Really sorry, boys, but I think I need to go home and chill, my heid's all over the place; think I'm having a bad trip? It's all been a bit much to deal with, if I'm honest, what with those alien radges back at the Peggy gig and those Banana Split cunts threatening to show up at Danny's, I feel really spooked with it all, and don't tell me that wasn't Dowpy's ghost, because I think we all know what we just saw there, right?" There was a look of pure torment in his eyes; I could see he was fraught and struggling to keep it together.

We stood still, looking at each other shivering in the bitter cold; there was a sense that at any moment The Fear was going to kick in big time! Either that or Dowpy would step out of the shadows and haunt the fecken bejesus out of us all. The very thought of seeing him again terrified me. I was scared.

The Daffy Ducks were kicking our arses, and we all knew it. Tony was nodding in agreement, "Aye, Fergus is right, we shouldn't be putting ourselves in danger a way oot here in the pitch darkness while we're in this state of mind, I think I'm going to head off home too, sorry, Danny mate; I need my bed before things get any weirder, I'm starting to lose my heid here. I need a wee lie doon." Before I could even respond they were all jumping ship and making their excuses to head off home, all of them looking anxious, the blotters were much stronger than any of us could have anticipated. This wasn't fun anymore.

"Ach, come on, boys, yer not going to leave on my own in this state of mind, are you?" There was a stony silence; it was obvious that they were all losing the plot, "Thanks very much, ya radges, I thought we were a fucking team, eh?"

One by one they all shook my hand and apologised, but it was clear that the mood had changed. *Maybe they're right, maybe I need to be on my own, the party's over, time to let the drugs wear off and get off to my own bed,* I thought. I looked at Jerry who was swinging his arms like a madman again, while the others started to wander back toward the town. "You abandoning me as well? Radgie boy."

Jerry stopped swinging his arms and gave me a nod, along with that unhinged grin of his. "I'm feeling a bit peckish, mate, think I'll head back into town and see what's about for eating."

"How can you even think about eating in this frame of mind? Ya nutter," I snapped at him. The very thought of food made me shudder inside, and I don't mind admitting that I felt a bit let down that even Jerry was going to forsake me. He gave me that kooky smirk one more time, and then ran off into the darkness to catch up with the others.

Great! I thought, as I stood there feeling miffed by the sudden change of heart by everyone, *even my dearest pal, radgie boy - Jerry deserted me. I hope he doesn't do anything stupid, the daft bugger!* I was starting to admit to myself that things had gotten a bit too weird, as I wandered off in the other direction, afraid that Dowpy was going to grab me by the throat at any moment.

Finally, approaching the path that led up to my house, I spotted the severed rabbit head that was still resting in the same place. There was a real sense of foreboding as I walked up to it, but I couldn't help myself, I was compelled to look for a brief moment wondering if there could be any truth in Chong's theory of this being the work of Satanists. *Satanism my arse! The work of bored teenagers, more like!* I told myself, but just then I remembered the image of the bunny head on the silver platter spitting yellow bile at me. *Stop indulging in your fear, Danny, you're tripping out, mate.*

I stomped onwards at a pace to get back indoors to some warmth away from the clutches of the cold, and away from the strange atmosphere that was overwhelming my senses.

Walking up the pathway toward my front door, I could see the neighbours were home, their curtains twitching like crazy. "Nosey bastards are at it again, I see," I muttered to myself.

After a bit of fumbling around trying to get the key into the door I clambered in. Thankfully, the heating had kicked in and for once my house felt warmish. I rummaged about to get the kettle on to make a cup of tea. *Builders' tea, with the teabag squeezed to the max, ah yes some normality at last.* My inner voice attempted to ease the panic thumping in my chest while I yanked my coat off and slung it over the chair. I needed to chill out and calm myself down.

Quickly I flicked through my records and put on *After the Gold Rush* by Neil Young, then I sat on the edge of the sofa and started sipping my tea, which still had that familiar crispiness, but I didn't care anymore.

There was still some Sputnik hash in the bong, and like a deluded fool I concluded that this would calm me down. Of course, I was wrong, the hash just brought on the hallucinations even stronger. The thing that I have learnt with tripping is that you hit a point where there is nowhere else to go, you have to make your peace with it, and let nature take its course by embracing the weirdness. I took another blast on the bong and then closed my eyes. It was all too much for me tonight, I needed to lie back and let the trip wash over me and surrender to the void . . .

Maggot Brain . . .

Where there are humans there will be flies. Where there are flies there will be maggots. Where there are maggots there will be death. I send you all three, 13 times!

1. Flies, maggots, and death!
2. Flies, maggots, and death!
3. Flies, maggots, and death!
4. Flies, maggots, and death!
5. Flies, maggots, and death!
6. Flies, maggots, and death!
7. Flies, maggots, and death!
8. Flies, maggots, and death!
9. Flies, maggots, and death!
10. Flies, maggots, and death!
11. Flies, maggots, and death!
12. Flies, maggots, and death!
13. Flies, maggots, and death!

Bursting the Bubble

All I can see is a beautiful, and when I say beautiful I mean, the most magnificent rainbow-coloured bubble that I have ever seen! Every atom within me is transfixed as it floats gently through space and time in a beautiful vacuum of pure nothingness, its perfect rainbows move like oil on a mini Jupiter. It comes closer and closer, eventually stroking me on the end of my nose like a feather.

There is no warning, it explodes like a nail bomb in my face; the detonation goes off in a strange lingering movement for what seems like an unbearable eternity. My life stretches out before me like a queasy cartoon full to the brim with dodgy karma, reeling over and over the mini dramas that seemed so irrelevant to me at the time. My head jolts back and bashes off of the wall next to the sofa.

I must have nodded off to sleep or something? Looking over at the clock: three am. A surge of wooziness coursed through my body, I needed to be sick, but I worried about opening the back door, *would such drastic action reveal a chamber of horrors? The thought scared me. Even if it does, there's a reasonable chance that I'll just puke all over it. Ach, whatever, who gives a shit, either way, fresh air is what I need!* Courageously, I opened the fucking thing. Instantly, the wooziness faded as I sucked in a few deep breaths of the cold night air. A phony sense of bliss heaved through my chest as the rushes kept coming on stronger and stronger.

I stood at the backdoor scanning the horizon as the moonlight reflected on the snowy fields giving them a stunning blue radiance as the dark silhouette of Harold's Tower stood out on the horizon a few fields away. I tried to pick out its four towers. The only thing I knew about the strange medieval burial vault was that it wasn't actually medieval at all, but was built by Sir John Sinclair of Ulbster before 1780 and that it sits where an older chapel once stood. This small segment of information was acquired from a book of local history that I randomly found on a seat next to me on the Inverness to Thurso train a few months ago when Alison and I were on a Christmas shopping trip.

The only other bit of information I knew of this strange building was written on the plaque on the SW side of one of its walls bearing the words: 'the burial place of the Sinclairs of Ulbster. Visited by OS (E G C) 18 April 1962.'

Apart from its history and purpose, this was also a place where I played as a young lad when out wandering, but these days it was the view from my kitchen window; where I would stare out at it while washing the dishes.

The snow was coming down again as I looked outward across the fields - we didn't have a garden as such; just cow fields. However, tonight there were no cows, tonight these fields were covered with a beautiful blanket of luminous blue snow that sparkled like a mini Antarctica. Something triggered in me and I got really panicky about those dodgy fucks The Banana Splits; I really didn't want to deal with those fat fuckers at this time in the morning, *why did Fergus put this idea in my head, why? Why can't they go round to his house, eh? Why is it always me they seem to pick out? Fuck sake.* My heart beat like a hammer; the rushes were getting more and more intense - I needed to do something - something primal - something to snap me out of this speeding malaise!

Ach, what the hell! Ripping at my clothes I took another deep breath of frozen air into my lungs and started thumping my chest like an ape and before I knew what's what I was off running as fast as I could go, further and further into the darkness.

Now, if you've never taken a quick sprint into complete darkness I can assure you that it is one hell of an exhilarating sensation! But, to run into complete darkness, bollock-naked, and into a heavy snowstorm, while tripping out on a cocktail of psychedelics *is* one mind-blowing hit to the senses. What was even stranger was that it seemed like my whole life was leading up to this one moment because somehow the absurdity of my microscopic existence didn't matter anymore. *This is it!* I screamed within myself over and over - *THIS IS IT!*

I kept running and running at full pelt, seeing nothing except snowflakes and darkness as the cold ate into my skin. I just kept running and running, beating my chest screaming, "UG, UG, UG, FUCKING - UUUUG!" over and over until I fell awkwardly, yelping with the shock of my bare arse hitting the snow at speed. Laughing like a madman while sprawled out on my back, looking up at the dark sky as the snowflakes fell even faster onto my face and body. I was overwhelmed with gushing feelings of love, which assured me that despite all the lunacy in my crazy messed-up life - there was still a glimmer of hope! *Am I ready to die; is this it?*

The cold ate into me and the shivering became unbearable. Common sense prevailed and I decided to cut the hippie shit and get back indoors before hypothermia kicked in; *I'm not ready to die, well not like this, no, not like this.* Staggering to my feet I made my way back to the light of my backdoor.

That's when I spotted it. A weird numbness took hold, but this wasn't from the biting cold, I was way too terrified to care about that anymore. The rabbit's head was sitting on the back doorstep; pure dread set in and I was suddenly panic-stricken, and utterly terrified. All I could do was stare at it; dread rinsed through me. Then, that unmistakable smell of stale tobacco whooshed around me like a cloud of sleeping gas, I spun around staring back into the dark fields. I knew at any moment Dowpy could step out of the darkness as I kept looking around, terrified, then I noticed in the light being cast from the doorway that the snow was completely covered in . . . *rabbit droppings?* It was everywhere; the fields were covered for as far as my eyes could see!

The grumbling voice of Dowpy boomed around me, exactly like it had done earlier on, but this time it was moving about much faster. Part petrified, part spaced out and totally disorientated I tried to rationalise what I'm seeing - *rabbit droppings - everywhere?* Then I got another face full of horrible tobacco smoke. "I know you are out there, Dowpy, what do you want with me?" Yet again, I got another face full of rancid pipe smoke and then that familiar retching sound he would make with his throat, followed by the familiar sound of his repulsive spitting.

Of course, this scared me half to death and I ran back into the house, but in my panic the rabbit's head got wedged in the door, so I grabbed it by the ears, yanking it into the kitchen and then slammed the door shut, freaking like crazy with the backdoor key to get the bastard thing locked. The key turned, I stepped back from the door. The doorknob started shuddering and rattling like the fucker was trying to get in, then there was a - BANG, BANG, BANG - the doorknob rattled once again. I screamed out, "GET THE FUCK AWAY FROM MY DOOR, DOWPY, OR I'LL PHONE FOR THE POLICE AND GET YE LIFTED!" The smell of tobacco gradually vanished.

Then the thought crossed my mind that it wasn't the police I needed, it was a fucking exorcist that was needed here! The rabbit's head dropped out of my frozen grip to the floor. "I don't believe in ghosts, I am hallucinating, ghosts don't exist, Danny, ghosts aren't real!"

Then it happened and all I could do was scream and scream. My hands had turned into … RABBIT PAWS! I fell to my knees blubbering like a two-year-old lost in a shopping mall. "What's happening to me? Why am I turning into a rabbit? Why me? Jesus Christ, I'm losing my fucking mind!" I screamed out to myself.

There was more blubbering, as I kept telling myself to get a grip, trying to rationalise the situation. Finally I attempted to get my clothes back on. Not easy with rabbit paws, I can tell you! More time was lost; not sure how much, but time was lost, then some more blubbering ensued until no more blubbering could be done. It was like a death in the family as I sat there staring at my fluffy white paws. "Those Daffy Ducks have kicked my arse - DANNY, YOU ARE TRIPPING OUT!" I screamed.

Retelling myself over and over that it was simply - a bad trip! Still, I found it pretty difficult to make a cup of tea with rabbit paws for hands, but after a few attempts I soon sussed out the knack of it. Alison was due home on the last train from Inverness later that night. *I've got all of the afternoon to sort the place out, which gives me the whole morning to sober up*, I thought, observing the clock on the kitchen wall - It was five am Sunday; there was plenty of time to sort my head out. *I must not forget; she'll go nuts if she finds out about my little binge.* This prompted me to grab a pen and paper, I managed to scrawl the word: ALISON, in big letters, then I placed the bit of paper on the floor next to the rabbit's head.

I tried really hard to ignore the urge to look in the mirror. I needed to keep drinking tea and calm the fuck down, but there was no way I was putting the television back on in case those cunts the Banana Splits were on. I didn't want them invading my home with their evil powers, forcing me to partake in their crazy activities. My mind heaved at the very thought of it, as I hunkered up on the sofa holding my body tight, praying for the drugs to wear off.

Looking down I wondered why there was a piece of paper with the word 'ALISON' written on it. "Oh my God, why did I write that?" Then I stared at the rabbit's head for a moment and to my amazement a massive bluebottle crawled out of its left ear. Without any warning it flew right at me. Coming at me again, and again, buzzing louder and louder as I swung my rabbit paws around like fluffy hammers trying to get the fucker away from me. "Come on, Danny, get a grip of yourself, man, get a FUCKING GRIP!" I growled, realising how mental I was acting.

Then I heard it - "Buzz, buzz, buzz." The fly zipped around, getting more and more frustrated, momentarily landing here and then over there, crawling on the coffee table, then flying off again and landing sideways up on my mug. I swear it was the size of a golf ball! "Ya filthy bastard, I'm gonnae squash you, ya wee cunt!" I growled to myself through gritted teeth, while slowly rolling up one of Alison's glossy fashion magazines to swat the fucker. Next thing I know I'm running around the house swiping at the fly, but it was no good, it was way too fast for me. In fact it was like the bugger was totally up for a scrap, coming at me like a wasp or something.

Erratically I panicked, screaming like a little girl, dropping the magazine and hiding under a cushion behind the sofa, it still kept coming at me. *This isn't normal, those cunts are only supposed to live in the summertime; this is the middle of winter?* The Fear kicked in and I made a dash for the bathroom, terrified, slamming the door behind me; quickly locking it just in case. "Aye, maybe that's not a normal fly, aye, maybe those Banana Split radges have put a curse on me because I didn't invite them over for mushroom tea?" Then I heard it again, only this time it was on the other side of the bathroom door.

"Buzz, buzz, buzzzzz."

My stomach started turning like a cement mixer full of liquid shite. It was too late; I fell to my knees and shit myself over and over, curling up from the diarrhoea pains. The lights went out.

Catching Flies

"Aye, ya cunt, I'll buzz, buzz, buzz, FUCKING - buzz ye, I'm gonnae stove yer fucking heid in, ya wee prick! Buzz, buzz, buzz, FUCKING, buzz, and then I'm gonnae wait till ye dissolve and go tae fucking goo. Aye, then I'm gonnae scatter my pheromones and gie all my pals the nod tae come doon tae the party, no. Buzz, buzz, buzz, FUCKING, buzz, and then the feast will truly begin!"

"Do ye hear me, cunty face? Aye, and by-the-way, don't think for a moment I cannae wait it oot, ya fanny, it's a pure myth that us hoose flies only live for a few weeks. That is a load of pure bollocks by-the-way, I've been alive for at least six months, ya dick! Do ye hear me, ya fanny? Buzz, buzz, buzz-FUCKING, buzz."

"I'm gonnae go pure mental if that dick doesnae open that door! Think yer clever, ya cocksucker, look at the state of this joint, fucking-well humming in here by-the-way, ya tinky wee bastard, buzz, buzz, buzz, FUCKING, buzz. Aye, just how I like it, ya dick!"

"It's, buzz, buzz, buzz, FUCKING, buzz, radges like ye that gi us flies a bad name, ken, buzz, buzz, buzz, FUCKING, buzz-actually if it waurnae fur us flies this world would be a far filthier place, aye, ken wha I mean? We recycle aw the shite yoos dicks fling oot! Aye, truth is sunshine, us flies are keeping the place clean, ya twat, ye. Withoot us cunts daein uir job there would be nae fucking frogs, lizards, spiders, bats, dragonflies, fish and birdies by-the-way. Buzz, buzz, buzz, FUCKING, buzz, aye, an' we fucking-well pollinate flooers as well I'll have ye know!"

"Aye, bet ye didnae ken that, ya twat, eh, eh?! Aye, and yoos cunts ur sprayin pesticides aw ower the place an' ye have the damn cheek to label us flies as filthy vermin? Buzz, buzz, buzz, FUCKING, buzz, I swear I'm gonnae go pure mental, open that door ya wee cunt, Buzz, buzz, buzz, FUCKING, buzz!"

"I'm gonnae spurt an' squeeze mah eggs aw ower yer hoose ya dick, aye, an' I hope my babies make your life a pure misery! Oh, by-the-way, it was the rabbit spirits who sent me and YOU'RE IN SOME DEEP SHIT, PAL! Aye, and yer mate is pure cursed, by-the-way, my wee wains are gonnae feed on yon cunt's deid corpse in a few days fae noo, aye, buzz, buzz, buzz, FUCKING, buzz!"

"Aye, I ken ye but ye cannae mind me, eh? I'm Prince, your uncle Hamish's dug, aye, I mind yon time you stood between me and that black bunny an near broke my fucking legs, buzz, buzz, buzz, FUCKING, buzz! Aye, noo I've been forced tae come back as a fucking fly, nae thanks to ye and yer uncle Hamish, pressurising me to kill all those bunnies and noo the rabbit spirits have sent me to sort ye oot, ya wee bastard, only then can I come back as a dug again."

"Aye, Danny boy, how far doon the bunny hole do ye want tae go?"

"Buzz, buzz, buzz, FUCKING, buzz, wonder what that cunt's daein in there? Buzz, buzz, buzz, FUCKING, buzz, probably having a sneaky wank, the dirty wee perv."

"That radge isnae hearing a word I'm saying? Buzz, buzz, buzz, FUCKING, buzz, must take a wee swatch at what I can puke on, aye, an' a may as well do a nice big jobby on one of the cunt's records, maybe lay a few eggs in his mugs. Aye, buzz, buzz, buzz, FUCKING, buzz."

"Had on, I'm getting the reek of shite coming from, buzz, buzz, buzz, FUCKING, buzz, behind the door; bastards taking a shite? Buzz, buzz, buzz, FUCKING, buzz, sneaky wee prick is sat taking a shite and I cannae get my chops aroond it because that fanny won't OPEN THE FUCKIN DOOR. WANKER! And here I am starving tae fuck, ya selfish bastard! Buzz, buzz, buzz, FUCKING, buzz."

"This is pure rubbish, ken. Bet the cunt is gonnae flush that juicy shite doon the toilet pan before I can get a wee Buzz, buzz, buzz, FUCKING, buzz, nibble, selfish dick! Buzz, buzz, buzz, FUCKING, buzz, I suppose I better have another wee chomp on some of that stinky bunny brains. It's nae my cup o'tea, tae tell the truth, buzz, buzz, buzz, FUCKING, buzz. Ach don't get me wrong like, bunny brains are actually a delicacy to us flies, ken what I mean? I'm nae that keen on it. I'd much raither suck up some of that fresh skitter I'm getting a waff of from funny-cunt's bathroom."

"Come on ya wanker, open the door and let me at that juicy keich, buzz, buzz, buzz, FUCKING, buzz, umm, smells so good, buzz, buzz, buzz, FUCKING, buzz, umm, smells, buzz, buzz, buzz, FUCKING, buzz, so, buzz, buzz, buzz, FUCKING, buzz, FRESH!"

"Had on, I can, buzz, buzz, buzz, FUCKING, buzz, get in the gap under the door, eh? Hoo comes I never noticed that? Ya wee beauty, here's hoping the fanny hasn't flushed that juicy keich doon the bog, ken. Noo, let's see if I can squeeze my wings under the gap, ach nae bother wi that, eh? Cunt's spaced oot tae fuck and, ya beauty, he's left his keks on the fluir covered in yummy skitters, nom, nom, buzz, buzz, buzz, FUCKING, buzz, nom, buzz, buzz, buzz, FUCKING, buzz-nom, nom, buzz, buzz, buzz-nom, nom, so FRESH!"

"Guid shit that, by the way, jist the ticket, ken. Had on, looks like fanny face is comin roon, I'm gonnae squirt a few eggs in his skitters cus these keks are deffo heading fur the bin, at least my wee bairns will grow and be in fine fettle, the wee fuckers may stand some chance of getting oan in life, buzz, buzz, buzz, FUCKING, buzz, ken what I mean. Aye, radgie I'm gonnae buzz, buzz, buzz, FUCKING, buzz-the-fuck OOT of ye, buzz, buzz, buzz, FUCKING, buzz, fucking-buzz, buzz, buzz, FUCKING, buzz, so fresh, nom, nom!"

Running into the Darkness

"Leave me be, PLEASE leave ME . . . what the fuck is going on with me? Och, och I'm covered in shite." Sickened with myself, I lay there watching the fly, circling around the room, wondering what the wee bastard's problem was, why pick on me, have I not already been through enough?

My stomach started doing cartwheels again. That unmistakable smell of my own shit hits the back of my throat, making me feel really queasy. I slowly became aware of the mess I was in. Crawling on my hands and knees, slipping about in the shit which had somehow seeped through my jeans and smeared all over the lino floor where I must have passed out.

The smell was awful. Any effort to puke in the bog was pointless; I missed the target, vomiting pink bile all over the wall and floor while making this pathetic yelping sound as each wave of puke flushed through me. Once the puking stopped I curled back into the foetal position again with the unrelenting buzzing of the fly vibrating inside my tormented skull.

There was no willpower to move, lying there like a sick pig rolling about in my own puke and shite as stomach cramps crippled me with stabbing jabs of pain. My innermost *me* was the only anchor of reality left; everything else seemed too disturbing to dwell on, *a person could go insane dwelling on heavy shit in this state of mind, for Christ sake!*

The thought of going insane forced me to stand up, while having to duck from the gnashing wings of the fly as it still raged around the room being gnarly as fuck with the light bulb, as well as with me. *Shame the bulb is such a low wattage; it just isn't quite hot enough to vaporise the fucker's wings,* the wicked thought resonated through me, while I clung to the edge of the sink. "Come on man, get yer heid together!"

The sound of my own voice snapped me out of the stupor so I started ripping my clothes off; my legs were gone as I opened the bathroom door and soared like a phantom into the bedroom. Briefly, I caught my reflection in the mirror; the one that hung from a rusty nail with mildew growing around it. *Stay away from mirrors, Danny; you know the rules!* I told myself and then for some reason pulled open the top drawer of the chests of drawers and grabbed a pair of pants, quickly pulling them on without really looking, more preoccupied with trying to coax my paws to turn back into hands again.

Stepping over to the window I pulled back the curtain, it was daylight outside but I had no idea what the time was, time just kept getting lost. At one point I broke down screaming for time to stop, at least until I could get my head together.

A fog of amnesia fell over me; I didn't have a clue what the hell it was that I'm blubbing about anyway? That's when I did a really stupid thing. I looked in the mirror. Who the fuck was that staring back at me through that horrible, horrible looking glass, you know - the one that hung from that nauseating rusty nail, that I hate so much, yes, the one with the fucking mildew growing around it! Part rabbit, part human, the results were disturbing and hideous beyond words. I grimaced back at my reflection, lost in the moment. A surge of fear crashed down on me like a tsunami and I started panicking, I looked back at my hands again; they kept morphing in and out of shape. "MAKE YOUR FUCKING MIND UP, FOR FUCK SAKE!" I stepped away from the mirror.

Calm the fuck down, Danny! What time is it? The sun was still shining outside but there were dark wintery clouds looming, then I spotted the small clock by the bed: four-twenty *in the afternoon, surely not, it can't be getting dark?* I closed the curtains, unable to cope with any more conundrums about time; it was too stressful trying to work it all out! *It should've worn off by now?*

The continual questioning in my scorched brain brought on even more questions, it felt like my head was about to explode like a massive jelly with a lump of Semtex sticking out of it. *Maybe I'll never come down from this! Maybe I am crazy! Maybe I've always been crazy?* I looked at my paws again, they looked real, and they felt real. *How can this be?* "Please give me back my hands, I don't want to be a rabbit anymore - PLEASE STOP THIS!" I ran back to the mirror again.

The reflection in the mirror was a disturbing sight to behold; I looked like a crazed lunatic with massive bunny ears and ridiculous oversized teeth. The fly crashed the scene, coming at me again and again. Yelping, I dived under the bed, petrified. Claustrophobia promptly set in, I was feeling suffocated in the small space, which made me panic and question, if in fact; I was actually under a bed at all? I became really troubled. *It feels more like a pit?* I couldn't piece together where I was exactly; my mind screamed for more answers. *I am under a bed, but whose bed? This is where I live, isn't it? Feels like I'm in a...warren!?*

My thoughts were interrupted again by the sound of the fly buzzing furiously around the room. *Something had to be done!* "That bastard fly is going to die!" The anger brewed up in me. "Buzz, buzz, buzz, FUCKING, buzz, I'm gonae KILL YE! Heh, heh... Buzz, buzz, buzz, FUCKING buzz. I'm gonae ... KILL YE!"

Smacking my head off the bed only fired me up even more, as I rose upwards like a King Kong bunny tossing the bed upside down. Looking around for the fly I noticed that the floor below me had morphed into a basin-shaped landscape with an evil jungle oozing out of it that throbbed with tiny life forms. None of this mattered as I swayed my giant paws at the shit-sucker.

The buzzing got inside me-buzz, buzz, buzz, FUCKING, buzz... then, randomly as you like, the shit-sucker zoomed out of the room. I watched it through the open door as it landed on the rabbit's head near the kitchen area, loitered for a moment, and then it crawled back into the bunny's ear. Quickly, I checked my hands; they were still paws. Looking around, I noticed that the house had shrunk. I caught my reflection in the mirror again; no longer was I King Kong bunny; more like Frankenstein having a stroke!

I floated through the shrunken door and levitated over to the bunny's head for a while. "Think you're getting out of here alive ya wee bastard, well I'm gonnae wait, heh, heh, aye, I'm gonnae WAIT! - heh, heh, I'm gonnae swish my arms, heh, heh, heh - faster, faster, faster, FASSSTER!" Swishing my paws, faster and faster at full power I laughed and laughed before breaking into song..."I'm late! I'm late! For a very important date! No time to say Hello, goodbye! I'm late! I'm late! I'm late! One banana, two banana, three banana, four - four bananas make a bunch and so do many more. Over hill and highway the banana buggies go . . . Tra la la, la la la la, tra la la, la la la la. Tra la la, la la la la, tra la la, la la la la . . ."

My massive bunny teeth clenched with rage as I stamped and stamped - and stamped, finishing off with a two-footed stamp, coming down on the bunny skull with the full power of my body weight. The pleasing crunch of the skull rupturing like a coconut being smacked with a lump hammer left an evil smirk on my face. My feet were all cut and oozing with blood; I don't care. I started swishing my paws again, as every atom in my body levitated off of the ground. I loomed over the crushed bunny skull like a drunk vampire.

Without warning there was the rattling sound of a key going into a lock. *I know that sound anywhere!* The door opened and all my nightmares came true. Alison stepped into the room; her face instantly transformed into that of a dead china doll. The massive suitcase she was holding with both hands slipped from her grip, falling to the floor with a dull thud. I looked at her then look back at the squashed rabbit's head, it was only at that moment I came to my senses and realise I was smeared in blood, puke and shit, wearing nothing but her tight fitting Bugs Bunny knickers, embarrassingly yanked up to my belly button. I stopped swishing my paws.

Alison stared at me; repugnance carved into her pretty little face, and then she glared over at the squashed bunny head sitting on the floor along with the piece of paper with her name scribbled in large capital letters on it. She started looking around the room as the smell of shit visibly hit the back of her throat; she heaved then let out a pathetic yacking sound while raising her hand over her mouth. She started sobbing uncontrollably while shaking her head at me. I looked down at the squashed remains of the rabbit's head and to my absolute astonishment the fly crawled out from one of the crumpled ears; somehow the fucker had survived the pounding I had given it.

"What have you done to the house, and why are you wearing my knickers and smeared in . . . is that shit I can smell? What have you done to your foot; it's covered in blood? Why is there a rabbit's head on the floor?" She looked around, horrified; the house was trashed.

"WHAT HAS BEEN GOING ON HERE, DANNY?" The appalling sight of me standing wide-eyed looking insane must have terrified the poor girl. Gazing down at myself I noticed that one of my bollocks was hanging out of the knickers, of course, I had absolutely no memory of putting these on. Without delay, I sorted my bollocks out covering them up. "I know what you must be thinking, but, but I can explain everything, please hear me out, please?"

Pleading for forgiveness was futile as I tried to explain that it was that wee bastard of a fly who caused all the trouble, as well as trying to put her in the picture about Fergus foreseeing that those antisocial cunts the Banana Splits were going to show up, who were, in my mind, most likely to be behind *all* of this. They were the ones who had sent the fly over to torment me and the only way to protect myself was to swish my arms like Jerry did at the Peggy gig, brewing up the power - at full power! But when I tried to explain to her about Dowpy coming back from the dead and trying to break into the house, and that my hands kept morphing into rabbit paws, she gave me a confused, empty look.

Although, deep down, if I'm honest, I knew that swishing my paws had indeed failed, but apart from these few minor setbacks it all made perfect sense to me and I couldn't for the life of me understand why she wouldn't accept this perfectly reasonable explanation.

I stepped forward to show her my rabbit paws but they had somehow morphed back to being hands again without me even noticing. "It's no problem, Alison, once I've killed the fly I'll get rid of the squashed bunny skull and it won't take long to clear up the empty beer cans and stuff." I looked at her for a moment. "I can explain everything if you give me a chance to sort this wee fucker out, come on now, be fair?" Alison stood there, looking at me aghast and then abruptly I projectile vomited pink bile all over the sofa not once, but three times. My dignity was shattered into a million pieces.

It's fair to say that she went fucking ballistic, and started flinging whatever she could lay her hands on at me. I stood there ducking like a drugged bunny man in a pair of ill-fitting knickers. Alison just kept screaming and throwing ornaments and empty beer bottles at me. Eventually, she calmed down, and started wandering around the house with her hand held over her mouth and nose. She started sobbing again and then the door slammed. She'd gone.

I struggled to understand what her problem was, and then I heard the - buzz, buzz, buzz, FUCKING, buzz, then - CLAP! Satisfaction rained over me as the gloopy remains of the fly was mashed into both of my hands. Pure carnal bliss rose within me as I gazed intently at the repulsive smear of black body parts mixed together with dark droplets of fly blood.

"GOT YE!"

Falling to my knees in front of the squashed rabbit's head I started weeping uncontrollably, "What, have I done, what have I DONE!?"

The comedown was truly awful, and I was riddled with guilt knowing that I had royally fucked everything up the arse - and then some! I fully accepted that Alison was never going to come back to me. No doubt she would tell all her annoying pals that I was a drug-crazed lunatic with a fetish for smearing myself in my own faeces while wearing women's knickers, as well as having strange urges to jump up and down on decapitated animal heads.

My heart sank at the very thought of it all, and the only time I ever saw Alison again was when she came over with her dad to pick up the rest of her belongings, which mostly consisted of a huge teddy bear and her creepy doll collection. I always hated those dolls with their painted-on faces and plastic eyeballs that followed you round the room. It came as no surprise that she had to tell her old man to stay in his car that day for fear of the cunt starting on me. Pathetically I pleaded for her to give me a second chance, but it was no good begging for forgiveness, she was having none of it. It was over.

A few days passed by curled up in bed with the curtains shut. I decided to move back into my mum and dad's house for a bit, where I spent a few more days curled up in a ball of self-pity, not leaving my room other than rushing to the toilet with sporadic bouts of diarrhoea; my liver felt like it had turned to chalk.

Even I had to admit to myself, that my life was a fucking car crash. Things would never be the same. My head was fried, but I couldn't help wondering why I hadn't heard from any of my pals, I just assumed they were all recovering, and like myself were all on a horrible come down. *Hopefully none of them had got up to any of the crazy stuff that I had! Just shows what drugs can do to a person, never again!* I told myself over and over, feeling the wait of the guilt and shame bearing down on me.

I decided to take a walk into town; the place was pretty quiet which was normal for this time of year. I keep walking and find myself wandering down by the beach; it was a cold day and the air felt fresh, but at least the snow was clearing up. By sheer chance I spotted my pal Cormag sitting with his legs dangling over the edge of the sea wall, which has a twenty-foot drop to the beach below. We nodded silently, giving each other a grunt as I sat myself down. I noticed he was smoking a spliff. "Do ye want a toke?" I tried to refuse the offer at first as he passed me the spliff. It didn't take much to talk me into it; I took a few long drags. It hit the spot instantly, giving me vertigo staring down at the drop between my dangling legs. I asked Cormag what he'd been up to the last few days. He shrugged his shoulders while staring out to sea and muttered in a very stoned fashion, "Nae much, just been watching the box and chopping up meat, you know work, work, work."

He looked up at me for a moment, "Aye, I heard a rumour that you and Alison split up, she's putting it around town that you went a bit nuts."

"Ach, I was getting pretty bored with the situation to tell the truth, it was too much pressure living with her, she was way too boring for me, and old before her time." I answered.

Cormag smiled; "Apparently you were caught wearing her knickers and doing something weird to that rabbit's heid, having a wank or something, that's what her pals are saying - ha, ha, ya wee pervert. Was it that rabbit's heid we found?"

My heart sank. "Fuck me it doesn't take long for stories to get around this place, eh?" I gave him a look, then carried on defending myself, "That's a load of lies, the truth is, I'm not too sure what the fuck I was up to, like yourself, I was tripping out of my mind on those Daffy Duck blotters and all the other stuff we took. That was some heavy shit, it took days to come down off of that, and I'm surprised I didn't end up completely insane!"

Cormag gave me another smile. "Aye, you're not wrong there, that was some heavy shit, although, unlike yourself, I had a great time, listening to music and watching horror movies!"

I took another long hard pull on the joint and we both stared out to sea chuckling to ourselves, knowing that we were crazy fuckers who knew how to party hard. Suddenly there was a voice behind us. "Aye, boy, what are you doing smoking hash at this time in the morning, ya wee fucking radgie?" We both turned around and look up; to my disappointment it was Cormag's nutty cousin Nibs dressed in a shiny tracksuit, and his girlfriend Tanya wearing a t-shirt with a picture of a candy pink cartoon rabbit giving the finger sign with the word 'Dope' written above it. Also tagging on behind them was her crazy alcoholic dad, 'Fat Sandy', who appeared to have his leg in plaster and was using crutches to hobble about with.

Of course, they sat down beside us, even Fat Sandy, who was pished out of his neep managed to dangle his broken leg over the edge of the sea wall. *Great!* I thought to myself as Nibs snatched the spliff from my hand, while cracking open a tin of Special Brew. He started ranting on about how he was trying to make the most of the next few days, seeing as he was about to do a five year stretch in the jail for breaking some kiddy's neck. I looked at him for a moment then politely asked him what happened. He told me it was because this kiddie tried to jump the queue at the taxi rank, and that it was his own fault for being so lippy.

Nibs was well known for being violent; he scared the living shit out of me. On the other side Tanya's dad was banging on to Cormag about his time in the army and how he engaged in battle in the Falklands War. Cormag was glazing over while secretly trying to avoid being hit in the face with all the spit and dribble spraying from the old alcoholic's mouth. This was one of those situations where my brain raced to find any excuse feasible to get away from these scary people.

Some pretty girls walked by on the beach below. Instantly a wicked smirk stretched across Nibs's ugly face, and then he muttered in a perverted voice, "Aye, pussy everywhere I look today." Tanya, who was sitting on the other side of Nibs, smacked him full on in the face, and then to my utter disgust she followed it up with a head-butt catching him on his left eye. "I fucking hate ye, ya cheating wee bastard, I hope ye rot in the jail!"

I got up quick-fast and took a few steps back as the pair of them rolled about on top of each other right by the edge of the wall; Cormag got up too and gave me the signal to split. Then, the crazy buggers both started snogging each other, wildly, it made my stomach turn watching the pair of ugly fuckers as they sucked on each other's faces. The old boy was pished out of his brains totally oblivious to it all and was still ranting away about the Falklands War as if he were talking to someone, even though there was no one there.

Cormag gave me another nod and we both wandered off, glad to get away from the bunch of nutters, I took a quick look back and they were still snogging. Tanya's dad had finished ranting and was watching on in silence, with a perverted smile on his face, as white foamy dribbles gathered at the edges of his horrible bearded mouth. I felt sick.

Cormag rolled his stoned eyes at me. "Jesus Christ, why do I have to be related to those inbred cunts, eh?" We grinned at each other, shaking our heads, and walked up the road to see if we could get a bag of chips for lunch, the munchies had kicked in big time. To our disappointment the chip shop was closed; it was still too early, and due to our stoned episode, and the fact that neither of us wore a watch we had no idea what the actual time was until reaching the town clock. It was only eleven-fifteen in the morning.

I offered to make Cormag a cheese toasty back at my folks' house, knowing that they were out getting the weekly shopping at the supermarket. We headed up Ormlie Road in silence; too stoned to say much, our minds preoccupied with food. As soon as we got indoors I fired into making some toasties for the both of us. This was a proper case of the munchies, devouring a whole loaf of bread, half a bottle of brown sauce and most of a block of cheddar cheese. Sitting on the backdoor step I looked over at my pal, who was sipping builder's tea out of my dad's Rangers F.C. mug while sitting on a plastic deck chair that was partly covered in a thin coating of luminous green moss.

Without giving it much thought I chucked the last crust of my toasty to the far end of the garden, and then out of nowhere two massive seagulls arrive on the scene. Cormag and I watched on as the seagulls started bickering over the piece of crust, at first they did the typical flapping of wings at each other, while puffing out their chests. But our eyes widened when the vicious pecking started. *Peck, peck, peck . . .* Then to our absolute revulsion one of the seagulls caught a tight grip of the other one's neck and started shaking harder and harder. It was exactly what a dog does when it's trying to kill a rabbit. Cormag gave me a silent look of bewilderment, a strange spectacle to behold; *surely this is not how seagulls normally conduct themselves, is it?*

Eventually the white feathery neck of the punier seagull started oozing blood, while limping and flapping its wings rather pathetically to escape over the fence into our neighbour's garden. The other seagull quickly wolfed down the morsel of bread and then flew away.

Hearing the front door opening I looked behind and saw Mum and Dad with shopping bags in their hands. I got up to help Mum with the heavy bags, as Dad stepped by me and out of the backdoor to say hello to Cormag. He needed a fag. I carried on helping Mum put the shopping away and once that was done we sat opposite each other at the kitchen table. Dad and Cormag were still outside chuckling away about the two seagulls. Mum quietly read the newspaper. All of a sudden a look of disbelief washes over her face as she slowly looks up at me.

"What's up, you look like you've seen a ghost or something?" I joked, wondering what the hell was going on. She handed me the newspaper. "I'm so sorry, Danny, I'm assuming you've not heard the sad news?" By now I was getting even more confused, I'd never witnessed my mum behaving like this before. My gaze was drawn straight to the photograph - *it was Jerry?* I read the headline: **Man found dead from a suspected heroin overdose.**

At first I thought there had been some sort of a silly mistake or mix up of identity; *Jerry wasn't a heroin addict. I would have known for sure if he was into that sort of shite, and I knew for a fact that he wasn't!* My mind raced for answers as I read on; apparently his body had been in the back of his van unnoticed for days. I double-checked the photo, but it was beyond any doubt; it was him! The police gave a statement declaring that: **A man believed to be in his early thirties formally known as Jeremy Swift of no fixed address was found dead** on Tuesday morning from a suspected heroin overdose. The alarm was raised when a dog walker noticed that a van had been suspiciously parked for a number of days in a secluded area close to Dunnet Head.

When the police arrived to find out who the owner was they noticed a buzzing sound coming from within the vehicle, it was at this point that the officers knew something wasn't right. The vehicle was forced open revealing the decomposing body of a young man, which was covered in flies. It is thought that the man had been dead for a number of days. The police found some drug paraphernalia, a small amount of heroin and some hashish resin.

After a thorough search detectives were surprised to find a decomposing rabbit's body with the head missing stuffed in the glove compartment of the vehicle. Also, a bin liner with thirteen decaying rabbit's heads was discovered hidden under a makeshift bed. Investigations are taking place in order to find out if this is connected to the spate of pet killings over the last few months around Thurso, as well as trying to shed some light on the chain of events leading up to this tragic misadventure.

My dad and Cormag stepped through the back door into the kitchen, oblivious to the situation. I looked at Cormag with tears running down my face and handed him the newspaper. He looked totally puzzled. "Jerry's dead," I muttered. Mum put her arm around me and with her other hand pulled a clean tea towel from the kitchen drawer to dry my eyes with. I couldn't stop crying, it was like a punch to the heart.

Cormag read the awful news in silence and then he looked at me and whispered, "No way, man, I can't believe this has happened - not Jerry, surely this can't be true?" My old man grabbed the paper from Cormag's hand and browsed through it, shaking his head in his usual self-righteous manner, doing his tut-tut-tutting thing, his way of expressing contempt, which over the years had really annoyed the fuck out of me. I knew what was coming next!

"Aye, what's the world coming tae, aw these druggies coming fae doon the line bringing their filthy way of living to uir toon; good riddance I say, bloody junkie bastard - killing people's pet rabbits like that; bleddy lunatic!"

Mum ushered Dad out of the kitchen before he could say another word shutting the door behind her. *This was no time for family squabbles.* I felt numb.

"Where do you think he got the heroin from?" I quizzed Cormag.

"Where do ye think he got it from; Chong of course!" he snapped back at me as if I were stupid for even asking the question. Shouting started coming from the other room as my mum and dad quarrelled with each other. Cormag looked at me as tears ran down his sad face, "Fancy going for a wee pint - droon our sorrows? It's on me."

"Aye" I muttered.

Down the Bunny Hole...

Unfurl let go - sacramental human soul . . . Further down the bunny hole shall you fall, fall, fall! No doors, no locks, no keys. No birds, no flowers, no sky, no trees. The harder you look, the further you fall, fall, fall! Deeper and deeper into the warren you must go. Welcome to the labyrinth of the sacred bunny hole.

Unfurl let go - sacramental human soul . . . Further down the bunny hole shall you fall, fall, fall! You tiny atom, you pathetic, insignificant mortal piece of nothing! The harder you look, the further you fall, fall, fall! Deeper and deeper into the warren you must go. Welcome to the labyrinth of the sacred bunny hole.

About the Author

I'm a slightly confused Irish-Scottish blend, born in Kettering, England, but brought up in Thurso, Scotland. After leaving school in the mid-eighties I drifted about in Glasgow, then moved to Bristol and stayed there for thirteen years. I have a BA Honours in Philosophy. I'm now living with my wife and three kids in deepest darkest Cornwall working as a writer of dark humour.

http://www.charlienewlands.com/

Printed in Great Britain
by Amazon.co.uk, Ltd.,
Marston Gate.